THE MAN FROM
BEYOND TOMORROW

ANTHONY C. SPENCE

Black Rose Writing | Texas

ISBN: 978-1-68433-668-5
PUBLISHED BY BLACK ROSE WRITING
www.blackrosewriting.com

Printed in the United States of America
Suggested Retail Price (SRP) $17.95

The Man from Beyond Tomorrow is printed in Calluna

*As a planet-friendly publisher, Black Rose Writing does its best to eliminate unnecessary waste to reduce paper usage and energy costs, while never compromising the reading experience. As a result, the final word count vs. page count may not meet common expectations.

THE MAN FROM
BEYOND TOMORROW

1

Tears began to form as Andrew Thompson knelt down at the grave of his friend and college roommate, Sean Wallace. He still couldn't believe he was gone. They had been physics majors in school and Sean had had the crazy idea of building a time machine. They had outlined the plans and were about to start building. He could still remember.

Sean Wallace was a tall, brainy guy who had arrived at school and immediately seemed out of place. Andrew knew how that was and when he saw Sean, they hit it off pretty well and decided to be roommates. Sean was always very positive. And even though they were both physics majors, they both loved history; Andrew loved American history while Sean was more into world history.

"Who would have thought," said Sean, "that two guys from different parts of the country would come together liking the same thing." Sean was from Oakland, California and had traveled across the country to Lighthouse College in Massachusetts.

"True that," said Andrew. "Nobody likes history. But here it is, we're going to be roommates and we like history. And when you think about it, no one looking like us in history got any respect."

Sean nodded. "You know, if we could go back and see some of the stuff in history that would be amazing. We would have to move very carefully because we could get ourselves in trouble."

Andrew laughed, "Yeah, they didn't like black people back then. We could give people a heart attack." He paused and stared at Sean. "Wait a minute, are you talking about a time machine?"

He could still remember Sean's sly smile when he said that. "That's it, Andrew," he said. "A time machine! We could build one."

"That's impossible. Science Fiction."

"Theoretically, yes. But it doesn't mean you can't try."

Andrew shook his head. "You're going way over the top now," he said. "Even Einstein didn't build a time machine. How are we going to build one? It could be dangerous time traveling."

"Absolutely, we'll have to be careful," said Sean, sitting at his desk and pulling out a sheet of paper. He was writing on it. "Einstein talked about time though. He thought it was possible. I need to write this stuff down before I forget." He wrote faster. "Just think we could be the first to cross the bridge of time."

"The bridge of time?" said Andrew. "You're not making any sense."

"Einstein said there was a bridge crossing over time and space."

"I don't know."

Sean jumped up and grabbed a hold of Andrew's shirt, staring into his eyes. "Listen, dude, I know you want to work for NASA. I believe they will still call you. Just think we could work on this around our schoolwork. We need to do the research but I'm telling you, it can be done."

Andrew looked into his friend's eyes and realized his heart was racing. "You're crazy," he said. "But it is interesting. We could go anywhere in time. We would need to figure out what we could travel in; a telephone booth, a car, or a refrigerator."

"All those have been done before."

"But Sean, if we do this, don't tell anyone about this. Not that anyone would believe us."

"You're right, this has to be a secret."

So they began the planning stage. They found a cylinder and began working out the math to open a way to allow the cylinder to be in another dimension. Andrew couldn't see how they would work.

"A cylinder?"

"Yes," said Sean, "it's better than a refrigerator."

"How are going to fit into this cylinder?"

"You're not thinking three-dimensional, Andrew."

"I usually have that problem."

Andrew realized that Sean was better at this than he was but he was learning and the framework was coming together.

Then on that night just before final exams that freshmen year, they had just left a restaurant in town on the way back to the dorm to study. They had been discussing the time machine and planning the next stage. Then Andrew heard a loud bang and people were running. Then another bang. Gunshots! He turned to Sean and didn't see him. He looked down and Sean was on the ground, bleeding. He knelt down by his friend, screaming.

"Sean! Do you hear me?"

Sean opened his eyes. There was blood oozing from the side of his head where the bullet hit him. "Carry on the work, Andrew," he whispered. "Don't tell anyone and open the portal."

"I can't do this without you."

"You have to. You have the data. I know you understand it. Tell my family I love them."

"Don't go, Sean," he cried. "We'll get you to the hospital."

"It's okay, man. Remember the bridge of time." And he died.

Andrew had gone to Sean's funeral in Oakland to mourn the loss of his new friend. He had never met anyone like Sean before, so full of life. He determined that he would make the time machine work and maybe he could go back and save Sean. Was it possible to stop Sean from getting shot?

Years later, there had been an argument over his dissertation at the University of Massachusetts. He had offered them more than words. Sean would have been proud of him. He had poured the passion of his theories into his proposal, had presented his facts and all the assumptions built upon those facts with a frenzied belief that one by one had seized the hearts and minds of every departmental official in his way.

One professor said the work he was doing was impossible and dangerous, another said it was his mentor, Alicia Stone's, work and not his own, but two others stood up for him. Alicia was there, of course, staring at the ceiling with her dark eyes, scribbling on her tablet PC, barely engaged in the argument. He sweated. Would she vote for him? But at the right moment, she raised her voice and said,

"Andrew is an excellent student, and more than that a fabulous physicist, a visionary. The ideas are completely his own. Now can you give him his doctorate so we can get back to work?"

And so he became a Doctor of Physics.

Andrew had thought about space, even inquiring about the United Kingdom's growing space agency. He contacted the United Kingdom Space Agency and spoke with Alistair Mackenzie, a friend of his he had met when he visited the agency not long before. This agency had replaced the British National Space Centre and began to develop space technology reaching for the future.

"Yes, Andrew," said Mackenzie, his gray eyes and smiling face looking back at him, through the video feed, "the agency is growing fast. We have expanded our satellite communications, Earth observation, disaster relief and climate control monitoring."

Andrew smiled. He knew he could make an impact. "I've seen on the vid links that the government is putting a lot of money into the space agency," he said.

"Yes, definitely that is true. By your dollars about 15.3 billion. The first spaceport just opened in the U. K., spurring the growth of space tourism, launch services and other things. We may even prove instrumental in Europe's new Galileo satellite navigational system."

"That really sounds fantastic," said Andrew. "I wish I could join your team."

Mackenzie shrugged. "I don't know what to tell you," he said. "We are making strides towards it, but we don't have any room right now to take on anyone else."

Andrew frowned, feeling deflated. "Okay, Alistair, I understand," he said. "I thought since our agency was kind of in-flux, I could try yours."

"It was a good idea, Andrew. I will sure keep you in mind. Don't give up. You never know what will turn up."

Andrew shook his head as the link disconnected. He knew that he shouldn't be discouraged. This was the way things were now. Spots were limited and so many people were out of work and looking. Besides, he knew that Alistair was a man of his word. If something came up, he would tell him about it. At least Andrew had the teaching job and it wasn't bad. He would have to be patient and keep checking the ads. Something had to come up soon. Yet, he thought, if he couldn't get there this way, maybe the time machine would be the ticket.

Andrew was working at a college campus nestled out in the country away from the bustle of the city. It was very New England, based in Massachusetts, about 40 minutes from Boston. Lighthouse College had been there since 1882 but it had been just a secondary school back then when it was called Beacon Academy. Then finally about 50 years later it became a junior college before becoming a four year college. The academy and college were separated with the two schools having their own buildings and administrations.

Now, Andrew Thompson, twenty-six-years-old, from Long Island, New York, walked the grounds confidently. He was six foot one and 190 pounds, a physics professor, and a doctor of astrophysics. He had a passion for science, especially for astronomy and he wasted no time in getting involved in everything dealing with space. The galaxy was a sea of stars and planets and other cosmic bodies. A sea, with a myriad of mysterious interactions and interdependencies.

He could have worked for NASA except that the space agency had been downsized. It wasn't being funded like it used to be. He had always loved doing research on space exploration in the applied sciences. It would have been exciting to live and work in that environment but there was also danger. There were only a limited amount of spaces available. Even though he was considered a whiz kid, he would have to wait for his opportunity. He remembered reading about another astrophysicist named Carl Sagan, who died back in 1996. He was a dreamer. It would have been great to have met him.

Andrew liked teaching and interacting with students. He had gone to the academy and afterwards the college and it was a privilege to be able to teach the next generation of thinkers. He wanted to inspire them to think big.

Not only did he love physics but his research had led him to work on a special project for the last eight years. His research had led him to explore time. He had researched this with Sean and now it was taking control. He studied string theory and metauniverses, and different dimensions. He looked at all the questions of what would happen in the stream of time if someone were to go back to change anything. He had explored the space agency's look at the space elevator and putting colonies on Mars. There was a ship that was headed to Mars a few years before but it was reported lost. There were four astronauts. No one knew what had happened to them. Also, it would be great to go to Jupiter or Saturn. There was even talk about wormholes that could lead to even more worlds to explore. What if going through a wormhole would lead to a world like Earth where resources could be used for supporting life? That would definitely be very exciting.

He had re-evaluated the physical universe and arrived at the conclusion that it was made up of matter and energy. He went a step further and figured out that it was already possible to convert matter into energy to achieve teleportation.

What if, he thought, what if this world, this universe that we perceive, is not all there is? What if it's only one of a number of infinite number of such worlds, such universes, not a universe in fact but of a multiverse, an infinite number of alternative realities and simultaneously occupying the same coordinates in space and time? And suppose the traveler was an access point to some kind of portal or vortex, whereby one could pass from one alternative into another, seeming in the process to disappear but in fact merely phasing into another dimension, another version of the story?

Change was coming.

Why a time machine? He wanted to witness the historical events in American history so he went about trying to figure out how he could construct a time ship to take him there. He told no one about this because he didn't want anyone to steal the idea and use it to destroy everything. He had read too many reports and seen too many bad movies that went along those lines. He would keep it under wraps for as long as he could.

Would he want to share this discovery with the world? Maybe one day he would. Then again, there was something to be said for keeping control over the conditions of the experiment. If he had done a public demonstration and people knew what he was doing, he would not be pulling the lever the next time. In fact, Lighthouse College's Center for Theoretical Physics would take it over and leave him out in the cold with no job and nothing to stand on. He knew he had to be careful and he had to conduct experiments to make sure it worked. He didn't want to go through the vortex and not be able to get back. He didn't want to end up with just half of himself or no way to breathe the air. There was still so much to do but he felt he was getting closer and closer to his goal.

Andrew was an only child and usually kept to himself. His parents were not scientists. His father was an auto mechanic and his mother was a teacher. They had always encouraged Andrew to pursue his dreams. They did not stand in his way in anything he truly wanted to do. And they were always there to celebrate with him. They sent him up to Massachusetts to stay with their friends near the school because they felt that Beacon Academy was a top-notch school that would challenge him. They were right. Andrew was a quiet kid who made good grades but didn't really have a social life.

2

Since Andrew saw himself also as an historian, he decided to research the history of the school. This also went along with the 150th anniversary celebration of the school's founding. He was going to write a book. All around him everything was being prepared for the big event.

The campus was being decorated in many different colors. There were programs, activities, speakers and other things planned for the event. Andrew didn't have an official part to play in the festivities but he went to some of the events anyway. Everyone was in such a great mood. There was so much excitement. The school had come through a lot over the last few years, as had the country. Now Lighthouse College was seen as one of the nation's best schools and enrollment went up a little every year. Plus, there was so much history here, not only for the school but for the community too. He wanted to do something for the school. He didn't know if his book would be ready in time for the anniversary but he wanted to try it anyway.

The students were excited about the anniversary. It was a big deal. Andrew knew that these events were good for the school. Sometimes even news trucks would be there doing video streams of the activities. Even the community became involved with the students. He shook his head in disbelief as he thought about it. Here he was thinking about the past but he had to put everything in its proper perspective. This was probably the best time to be alive, to experience this moment in time. Many of the school's founders would have liked to see his time too.

He researched the school back to its humble beginnings. There was only so much he could find using the internet and other video links. He went to the library and spent many hours looking over the old books and microfilms. They didn't even use this stuff much anymore. But he found valuable material that would be very helpful. He studied the founders, administrators, and students, who had a huge impact in the development of the school.

He would have to have a little more assistance on this. He had gone as far as he could on the resources that were available to him. He went to speak with the librarian.

"May I be of assistance, Doctor Thompson?" said Mr. Gray, the diminutive librarian.

Andrew smiled and was a little taken aback staring at the ghostly, glittering countenance of Ronald Gray, Lighthouse's librarian and archivist.

"I'm very sorry to disturb you, Mr. Gray," he said. "But I have a question."

"I see."

"An important question," he continued, a bit stupidly.

"Important. Well."

"May I speak with you privately?"

"By all means." He led the way into the whitewashed cubicle, furnished with cheap metal furniture because Ronald Gray did not hold with spending library money on anything but CDs and computer programs. Andrew sat across from him and spoke for several minutes, hoping he was making sense.

"You want to do what?" said Mr. Gray, thinking he was crazy.

"I need to do more research."

The man laughed. "In the archive area?"

"You keep copies of different books and newspapers here on that film stuff, don't you?"

"Doctor Thompson," said the little gray-haired man, shaking his head, "you know there are better ways to do research."

"I know, Mr. Gray. I've done that but I need the good old books. You still have the microfilms and videos from the 20th century?"

"Yes, but..."

"I need everything you have."

"Everything is in the archives."

Andrew smiled. "Then I will go there," he said.

Gray shook his head. "No one has been down there in a long time."

"I understand," said Andrew, carefully. "I'll dust the books and videos off for you."

The librarian stared at Andrew like he had lost his mind. The man shook his head. "Very well, Doctor Thompson, I will get everything set up for you."

Andrew went down into the basement to the archives section to do his research. He kept looking around, wondering if anybody were in the vicinity. He stepped into the alcove and thought he heard a sound behind him, but when he turned there was only the soft rumble of water in the overhead pipes, and the steady ticking of some unrepaired mechanical device in the wall. Mr. Gray was right, he thought, no one had been down there in a long time. The dust and cob-webs were everywhere. He sneezed. He sighed as he thought about what he had gotten himself into. He had to thoroughly clean the place before he could even start doing anything. Wasn't there any respect for history? Even the environmental robots refused to go to the basement. They were very particular about where they went every day.

When he had finished cleaning, dusting, and decontaminating, he searched every file and thoroughly entrenched himself into the history of the school. He was determined to write the best book he could write. If you're going to talk about and celebrate the history of the school, sometimes you had to get a little dirty.

Andrew quickly realized that there were no holographic displays that he could use and that it would have to be done the old-fashioned way. He went through the shelves and boxes being careful not to damage the contents of what he found. These things could be valuable.

People using these archives could switch on direct lighting to supplement the glow strips in the arched concrete ceiling, but not all the lights worked. Specifically, the area beside the desk where

Andrew was working didn't have working internal lights. The unsorted boxes within were lumps in shadow.

As he was doing his research from the archives and the many volumes of information, he came across a photograph of four girls from the class of 1888. Apparently, this was the first academy graduation class and he began researching who these four girls were. One of them, Rowena Michaels, had written journals and had published three books about the school when she became older. She looked like she was petite and had a pretty face. Because the photograph was in black and white, it was hard to tell what color her hair was. She was quoted many times in the book on the history of the school he was reading concerning many of the teachers and principals. After she graduated she became a teacher at the young school.

Sometimes Andrew was bothered by the degree to which he was oblivious of his surroundings where he was working, but he wouldn't accomplish nearly as much if he didn't concentrate. And it wasn't as though he had a choice: he was who he was.

Two of his friends, Russell Kingston and Keisha Ryan came by to talk to him. They didn't understand their friend's obsession with writing this book. Russell was a professor in the Education department and he loved the school. He came from Philadelphia and he and Andrew had become good friends. Russell was a big black man, six foot four, solid build, broad shoulders and a great smile. He had a few scars here and there from being in many fights as a boy, and boxing as a teenager. He had worked with intercity kids. He loved education and he wanted everyone to be their best.

Keisha Ryan was a professor in the Theology department. She was married and from Baltimore. She wanted to make a difference in her community by helping as many people as she could. Keisha was a tall black woman with lustrous features, short black hair, and a husky voice. She had an angular face with light brown eyes under well-defined eyebrows. Keisha and Russell saw their friend spending countless hours in the library down in the dusty and forgotten archives doing research for a book, not to mention the energy he would put into his classes. They were worried about him.

"Andrew, you need to slow down," said Russell, as he sat down next to him in the archives. Keisha sat across from them. "You're pushing too hard. You work late in the library every night. You're here till closing, sometimes later."

Andrew laughed. "What are you talking about, Russell, I'm fine," he said.

"And Andrew," said Russell, "you vanish from the face of the earth, you're hardly showing up for your classes, won't answer your phone, don't often answer your door. We're your friends, and we're worried about you."

"I go to my classes," said Andrew, "and I'm fine."

Russell shook his head. "You're a lousy liar."

"We don't want you to get burnt out," said Keisha.

Andrew sighed and asked Russell as if reading a script. "Is this the part where you tell me 'life is a brief window of opportunity, and today could be my last day here, and I should prepare for eternity, or one day I'll stand before God and wish I'd done something different?'"

Russell nodded. "I couldn't have said it better," he said.

"You shouldn't spend your life buried in the library," said Keisha.

"It's all good, Keisha, really. I'm enjoying this," Andrew said, pushing a book over to Russell. "Check out this photograph from 1888. This is the first graduating class at Beacon Academy. The girl on the right wrote and documented many things that happened in the school back then and she even went on to write a history of the school."

"I see," Russell said, looking at the picture and showing it to Keisha. "So, if there is already a book written about the school, why are you writing another one?"

Andrew sighed. "This is an old book," he said. "It's from the 1950s. In the 1980s, another guy wrote a book for the centennial. Now it's fifty years later. We need a little updating. Besides, with the anniversary coming up, it would be good to remember our roots."

"Your roots, my friend, you went to this school, I didn't," said Russell.

Andrew smiled at Russell. "But you're a part of it now."

Keisha shook her head. "Don't overdo it, Andrew. If you need help, let us know."

Andrew nodded, "I sure will."

"We love you, Andrew," she said. "Take it easy."

"Clearly noted."

Andrew knew they were right. Yet, he knew only one speed. He continued to familiarize himself with the past. He studied a map of the campus from the early days. He knew where every building was located and these included the buildings that were no longer standing. He was studying it so much he could have gone to school there and known how to get around. He was fast becoming an expert on the academy in the nineteenth century.

3

Andrew tried to make his physics classes interesting. It was so easy to have the same old dry classroom structure, the same type of lectures. In an age where everyone had a handheld device and so much information was at their fingertips, the old school ways were not done anymore. He still used the technology in the classes, but he invited interaction from his students who were among the best and the brightest. He had a class of twelve on this particular day which included a couple of online students on video screens. The subject was quantum physics and the discussion made a turn towards time travel.

"Doctor Thompson," said Marlene, a blonde, "do you believe we can travel through time?"

"Scientists say that is impossible, but it doesn't mean we should give up trying," said Andrew, thinking of what Sean had said while adjusting his holographic imager to show the outer space clip he was mentioning. "Remember that last year, the space agency said they had found a wormhole near Jupiter. I believe they are going to send a ship there to explore it. Who knows, it could take us to a new dimension, a new galaxy."

"It seems too dangerous," said Elena, a brunette.

"Wasn't there a ship, Doctor Thompson," interjected Marlene, "that was going to Mars that disappeared?"

"Yes."

"Could they have gone through a wormhole?"

Andrew nodded, understanding. "Interesting thought, Marlene," he said. "When you travel through a wormhole you don't just travel through space. You also arrive slightly in the future because you have traveled instantly while the rest of the universe is taking the slow route. This doesn't matter because when you travel back again, you go back the same distance into the past. And if you go the slow route, through space – well, no problem, you're still in the same time frame. So, it's impossible to create a paradox, like go back and kill your grandfather or whatever. But, open another wormhole too close to the first and potentially you could have a paradox. You go down one, back up the other and suddenly you're in the past, even if it's only a second. So that's why it's impossible to do so."

"Wow," said Marlene.

"Now we believe that our universe has a small extension in higher dimensions – higher, that is, than that of space and time we experience. But these extra dimensions are small."

"Dimensions?" said Elena. "Space and time?"

"Albert Einstein said space and time are flexible," said Andrew, as he worked the hologram image to bend as he talked, "that they can curve. Stars are massive enough to bend and stretch space-time sufficiently to create thin spots in it. Those thin spots are jump points that one day could allow ships to push into space towards the next star. If you can get a powerful enough gravitational field you could bend it back on itself, creating a kind of loop that would allow you a crossover to an earlier period."

An online student named Anita chimed in. "That's amazing," she said. "That would mean that the time zones are always there. You could communicate between time zones by sending messages."

"Sending messages?" said Jason, a dark-haired jock.

"Yeah," said Anita. "It would take a few years or decades but it could be done."

"Jason," said Andrew, "you look skeptical."

In fact, Jason looked uncomfortable. "It's hard not to be, Doctor Thompson. I can't believe people ever seriously thought they'd time travel around the galaxy. I know that's what we always say, but how does anyone really know that?"

"Read their books."

"Well, the fiction talks about time travel, but if you read the science abstracts of the period, I don't think you see much."

Andrew looked around the room. "Anybody want to respond to that?"

A young woman raised her hand. "It's because scientists are supposed to be ruled by the evidence. During the early years of the nineteenth century, there was no evidence."

Someone yelled out to her. "The early twentieth century, Danielle."

"Whatever. Their reputations were on the line, as they always are." Like Jason, she looked uncomfortable. She wanted to say more, but she smiled shyly and kept silent.

"What would happen if you went back in time?" said Andrew.

"You can see a lot of things from history," said Alex, a stocky fellow.

"There's always the possibility of changing something," said Elena. "Then when you returned to the present, everything could be different."

"Yeah," said Robert, a short black guy with glasses, "but what if you just went back to look? There's no harm in just looking."

"Don't step on a butterfly," said Jason.

"There's too much that can go wrong," said Marlene. "You may have all the good intentions in the world to do the right thing but just being in the past could change everything."

"What if you spoke with someone?" said Andrew. "You talk to someone or save someone's life or do anything in the past that didn't happen before and that changes the future."

"That's what I said before," said Robert. "Better to just go back and look around. If you talk to someone or do something that didn't happen the first time, it could cause all types of havoc in the future."

"You could change life for the better," said Alex.

"Or the worse," said Marlene.

"I have to agree," said Rachel, a pretty Spanish girl. "I don't think it's possible. The only thing closest is when you go near the speed of light and time slows down in the spaceship. But then everyone back on earth keeps going and aging and when you return, you're still young and everyone else is old."

"That would be really cool," said Jason. "Take a spin around the sun and you could be time traveling, or go through that wormhole they found and who knows where you'll end up."

"This is really fascinating," said Andrew. "I didn't know you were all so knowledgeable about time travel. I like the subject myself."

Space time had always been interesting. Time travel was always impossible. Of course, there was also the talk about alternate universes. Three were several versions of this theory, all based on different notions of the underlying structure of space time, but the most popular ones were. Many Worlds, Multiverse, and Bubbleverse. They all basically stood for the same idea, though: that time travel between separate universes was the most likely scenario. That was something he still had to explore.

Andrew was happy for the discussion. He didn't tell anyone that he was secretly working on a time machine. He welcomed the discussion because it gave him ideas he could use in his project. Who knew what would really happen? If he couldn't get out into space and search for that wormhole, maybe he could create something in his lab. Maybe he could change the future forever.

4

Andrew had been working on this machine for eight long years. People would think he was crazy to think of such a thing. It was impossible. Yet others had tried it. Albert Einstein, of course, had the theory. He said there was a fourth dimension. There was always, what if? No one can travel through time. Once time has passed that was it. Time passes into history. You couldn't go back and look at or change anything. He worked at it in his free time through college and even into graduate school and doctorate studies. He had to find the answer. There had to be a breakthrough just waiting to be found. He was happy to get a teaching job at the college he graduated from and his own laboratory where he could do his research in peace. He would spend many hours tinkering with the device to see if he could get it to work.

He had set up his computer with an artificial intelligence to work out the mathematical equations. He named it Jennie and gave it the female voice to match. It worked day after day with equations pushing him closer to his goal. It was almost non-stop. Jennie would alert him to any problems and he felt he was getting closer. He pondered what it would look like and what he would do. Nothing would detain him from his goal. It had to work.

He wanted the ship to be a device that could change with its surroundings. It would be able to change its outward shape to match what was around it. It would also be a ship that would be bigger on the inside than the outside. He developed an interdimensional stabilizer that would be part of the ship's mechanics. In this way, he could work on the inside of the dimensional vortex and make everything more comfortable for him. It was incredible how it happened. When he made the calculations and put it together, the results knocked him off his feet, literally. He had tapped into another dimension.

It was a sphere, an armillary sphere with metal bands spinning around it. It looked like the sun but the energy from it had incredible heat. He had tapped into something incredible, something dangerous.

He spent so many hours on this that it almost made his head spin. When the initial experiments worked out the changing of the structure of the ship, he was amazed. Now he was getting somewhere. He stabilized it and it expanded. Yet the simulations were one thing. He would have to take a field test to make sure that the simulation would hold once he reached and established his destination.

Andrew had to figure out how he would shape the ship. How would he survive inside the cylinder? He would need to have breathable air. He couldn't use oxygen masks during the journey. He would need to make it more livable so he could work in there. There would obviously be a lot of machinery and wires and other computer systems inside behind the scenes. He didn't even think of the dangers, he just pressed forward toward the goal. He knew the theory of curved space time. It could shift and bend back on itself, meaning he could go back and interact. But the tricky part in doing that was not only in getting there but making it back to the present safely. He didn't want to be stranded in time, especially the past.

He didn't have any social life so to speak. He was working all the time. He would come to work early and stay late, but he made sure he was able to teach his classes. He didn't want to neglect that. By all means, he had to make it appear that he was a professor, which he was. Yet he didn't want the job to interfere with the project. If it worked, it would change everything. He put in safeguards and security protocols so that no one could access the systems but himself. He worked out plans for secondary protocols in case something went wrong. He made four bracelets for communication and teleport capabilities. He put a trans mat terminal in the lab and in the ship. He also expanded the inside to include other rooms. He was the only one who would be able to operate the ship. He did not want it to fall into the wrong hands, not the college and especially not the government.

He was used to being alone. He would have liked to have had a relationship, but he just didn't pursue one. It gave him time to work on his time ship. He was able to focus on it and get it done. No one else would understand why he was doing this. His parents didn't even know about it.

How could he tell them that his ability militated against finding that perfect someone whom he might trust and love? Always, on meeting seemingly pleasant and beautiful women, he'd find them not always honest, leaving him disappointed. He didn't have time for those kinds of games. It was easier to absorb himself in his work, his students, and in the time machine to keep a tight rein on his emotions.

5

Yet his friends didn't give up. They would not let him just live his life in peace. Andrew's friends had set him up on a date a few weeks back. He didn't want to do it and thought it was crazy. But he couldn't get out of it. Apparently, there was another professor named Maria Salazar who liked him and wanted to go out with him. The prospect of a date seemed to him like a case of bad timing in several ways. But it also seemed like a good idea. He realized it had been awhile since a girl had been interested in him in a non-professional sense. His friends learned about this and set it up, knowing that Andrew wouldn't do anything on his own. He picked Maria up at her apartment and they drove to an Italian restaurant in town not far from the campus.

They were escorted to a cozy little booth in the corner. He noticed that heads turned as he and Maria walked across the dining room. There was even a table with four black women who turned and looked at them like they were aliens. Andrew thought it was probably directed at him because black women usually had a problem with black men being with non-black women. It was amazing that even in these days people still thought that way. Women were amazing creatures – sweet, soft, gentle, and far more savage than men were. His hands were sweating and he really didn't want to be there. He had too much work to do. He needed to get back to his lab, where he could continue his work undisturbed, without the interference of unimaginative people. Between his regular class work and his private project on the time machine, he barely had time to sleep.

He had never seen her looking like this, all dressed up, and she was even more beautiful than he had thought. She had on a long black slip dress that showed off nicely toned shoulders. A cream-colored shawl fringed in black lace was draped over one arm. She also had on black flat-heeled pumps.

But Maria Salazar was looking rather nice. She was a petite Latina, a professor from the nursing department. She had spectacular dark eyes with long lashes and a slight tilt to them, and a straight nose that made an open Y-shape against her brows. Mexican-brown skin, high cheekbones framed by thick black hair that shone navy in the light. Her skin was smooth and clear, the color of dark honey with a translucent glow behind it.

"Maria, I should have told you sooner," he said, as they sat down, "but you look great."

"Thanks," she smiled.

"Have you been here before?"

"I think I have once," she said, looking around. "I'm not really sure. Have you?"

"I don't think so. It came extremely well recommended," he said, and then added, "No one talks anymore, Maria, everything is done through a handheld device."

"True, talking is a lost art."

"I've been very busy in the lab, lately."

"Yes, I've noticed," she said, nodding. "Are you working on a special project?"

"Yes, I am," he said. "Did Russell tell you I needed to get out more?"

"Yes, he did. He said you were working a lot. He's concerned about you."

"I know he meant well. He's a good friend," Andrew said. "What's happening with you, Maria?"

Andrew was something of a loner, not much for casual talk, but conversation with Maria proved to be surprisingly easy. He had seen her around campus and had wanted to talk with her. Maybe he wasn't entirely blind to other people. He noticed other women and he saw Maria as she moved around the campus. He may have mentioned it to Russell which was why he was now in this situation.

"Nothing much for me, I've been working hard too."

At that time, the dark-haired waitress came by to get their drink orders. He figured that they had better look at the menus. While they were looking for selections to eat, he peeked over at her from behind the menu and smiled.

"So you're working hard too?" he said.

"Yes, I guess, we both need help."

The communication drew him to her. Very articulate, well-read, up on all the political activities in the neighborhood. Neither of them wanted to end the conversation. More like she didn't want to stop talking. Women always make it easy on a man. If you think about it, the secret of conversation is to get a woman to talk, then listen and absorb. They'll tell you everything. All you have to do is pay attention, nod your head a little and when she's through, repeat the last thing she said.

After they ordered their food, she looked over at him, and smiled. "You really had an interesting discussion in class the other day on time travel. The students were talking about it for the rest of the day."

He nodded. "That was an interesting discussion."

"I guess it was exciting to them because of what you said to me earlier about the handheld devices."

"Yes, I didn't expect the discussion to go that far. I encourage discussions in my classes. I have been very interested in the aspect of time," he said, pausing a bit to gather his thoughts. "If it were possible for you to go back in time and change something, what would it be?"

"Personal or otherwise?"

"Doesn't matter."

Maria thought a moment. "If I could, I'd do something about making sure my mother took better care of herself. She died of cancer when I was thirteen. The doctors could have saved her, if she had told someone."

"I'm so sorry, Maria."

"If she would have said something, we may have saved her. So if I could, I would."

Andrew was thinking that if this time machine thing worked, he could probably open up to Maria and take her back. She could save her mother and possibly change her future. Could it be possible? He had to finish the project. It had to work.

6

They were engaged in polite conversation as they finished their meal and the waitress came up to the table and asked, "Would you like to see the dessert menu?"

Andrew glanced over at Maria, who frowned and shook her head. "No, thank you," he said. "Could we have the check, please?"

Andrew was told by Russell that there was going to be a party over at his apartment that evening. He wanted him to bring Maria along after their restaurant date. Andrew said he would see how things worked out. After dinner, they took a walk.

"Have you always been so driven?" said Maria.

"I've always been working hard on something," said Andrew. "Can't help it."

"I guess your friends want you to settle down."

"Or slow down."

"True," laughed Maria.

He always liked her laugh. He had often heard her laugh. She wanted to suppress it but it came out anyway. A laugh that was always spontaneous, never self-conscious. She didn't notice and didn't seem to care if people turned and looked, as if a laugh was never something to apologize for. It was the laughing of someone who enjoyed life. He could tell why she was a very popular professor with the students. Maybe this date was not so bad after all. She was definitely a very nice person.

"I've always wanted to go into space," said Andrew, sadly. "I have a degree in astrophysics, but I never got the chance. I've even catalogued stars and studied the planets."

"The space agency is not altogether stable," said Maria. "Especially since America let go of the space shuttle program so many years ago."

Andrew nodded. "I thought about going over to the British space agency but spots are not available right now. I guess I'll just have to wait it out."

"What about private rocket companies or the space center itself?"

Andrew thought for a moment. "Yes," he said, "I have looked into those too, but so many people are looking for work and the competition is unbelievable. I need to be patient. I believe my time will come. I know it."

Andrew stopped and looked across the street into the shadows. Something rustled in the bushes across the street. He squinted into the darkness to see what was there. He felt a little tickle of awareness, as though someone was looking at them. He tried to focus in on the spot. Maria noticed him looking that way and glanced over.

"What is it?" she cried.

Andrew shook his head. "I thought we were being watched."

"What?"

"Someone's out there, Maria. Standing nearby in the shadows to our right," he whispered to her. She didn't look in that direction.

Maria's eyes grew wide. "Are you sure, Andrew?"

"I'm sure. Trust me on this one."

"Could it be Russell, or one of the others?"

He shook his head. "That would be nice," he said, "but I don't think so. This is entirely someone else." Then he looked at her. "You wouldn't have a jealous boyfriend, would you?"

She shook her head. "No, not me."

The man was watching just a few yards away from the nearest light source. He was dressed in black but he was there. Watching.

Why? Andrew could tell that the man was of average height or a little taller and looked lean.

As Andrew watched, the man turned, walked a few steps and vanished into the darkness.

Andrew shivered. He didn't like the way this was going. "You want to go to the party at Russell's place? Let's get out of here."

7

Andrew and Maria talked about the strange intruder on the way to Russell's apartment. He kept thinking about why someone would be watching them. If not Maria, then it was him. But why? Was it about the time machine? Did someone already know about it?

"Why would there be someone watching us?" said Maria.

"Someone may have been watching me."

Maria gasped. "Why?"

"It's the project I'm working on."

"What project? What are you working on?"

Andrew sighed. "I can't tell you about it yet," he said. "But if someone knows about it, I could be in a lot of trouble."

As they drove up to Russell's apartment, they could hear the music. The party goers were having a good time inside. He helped Maria out of the car by taking her hand and they went arm in arm up to the building. He still felt good that Maria was with him. He really liked her. As he walked, he wondered if he was still being watched. What was he going to do?

Music rolled and thumped inside while they waited at the door, and Andrew wondered what Russell's neighbors thought of this. Yet, knowing Russell, he probably invited his neighbors to the party. Andrew had to knock twice more before the door finally opened.

A pretty woman somewhere around her thirties answered the knock, and a tide of loud music came with her. She was maybe five-foot-six and had brown hair.

Her face lit up with an immediate smile. "Andrew, how wonderful to see you. Russell said you were coming by."

"Thanks, Rhonda," he said, and turning to Maria. "And this is Maria Salazar."

"Good to meet you, Maria. Come on in."

They walked into the apartment and the music was pulsating. There was classic rhythm and blues, and other alternative sounds. People were dancing and milling about talking. The place was packed. He even saw Keisha dancing with her husband. He saw some of his other friends who had helped to get his date. Sheila, Simon and Damon called out to them when they came in. Everyone was in a good mood. Even professors had a good time, Andrew thought. He needed to find Russell and talk to him though about his experience. He spotted the tall man up ahead talking to two people.

"Hey Russell!" he called.

The tall man looked over and acknowledged him.

"Maria," he said, "I have to talk to Russell about something. I'll be right back. Okay?"

"Okay, Andrew." He could see the terror and unsteadiness in her eyes.

He didn't want to leave her but he needed to let Russell know about the strange man. He had not told Russell about the time machine but his friend would still have an idea of what to do.

"I have to talk to you," Andrew told Russell. "It's important."

Russell nodded and led Andrew into the bedroom. It was a modest room with a couple of paintings on the wall. The bed was made and everything looked clean. "What's up?" said Russell. "How's the date going?"

"Listen, man, I think I'm being watched."

Russell stared at him. "By whom?"

"I don't know."

"Why?"

"I don't know that either."

"You saw this guy?"

"Barely, he was hiding in the shadows," said Andrew. "White man. He looked like he had blond or sandy hair. He was dressed in black."

Russell shook his head. "Are you sure you're not being paranoid?"

"I'm sure of it," said Andrew, frantically. "I didn't imagine this. Maria saw it too and she's scared. I'm scared."

Russell smiled shyly. "What are you doing?" he said. "Is it something illegal?"

"No, I'm not doing anything," said Andrew. "Do you think Winston has anything to do with this?"

"Doctor Winston is your department chairman. Why would he have you watched? Would he suspect that you're doing something illegal against the school?"

"I'm not doing anything. Keep an eye out for me. Let me know if you notice or see anything suspicious. He's bound to appear again. We'll need to know who he is and what his angle on me is."

"No problem, buddy," Russell smiled. "I'll see what I can do."

Russell did not have a girlfriend at the moment but he had been trying to romance a girl named Tracy. He tried for six months to get her to notice him. She had noticed him and they had gone out together. Russell pursued her hard and spent a lot of money. There was talk that she had two boyfriends but he still went out with her. He would have gone to the end of the Earth for her but it was not to be. They parted ways and Russell just wanted to get Andrew set with someone.

Andrew took a deep breath and smiled. "This looks like a great party. I better get back to Maria."

"You got that right, buddy," said Russell. "You two getting along good otherwise besides this other thing?"

Andrew nodded. "So far, so good."

Andrew found Maria sitting alone at a table in the musically enchanted room filled with people who were living in the moment, and nursed a soft drink while she bopped her head with the beat of the music. She was also occasionally snapping her fingers. He moved over to her to belay her fears.

"How about a dance?" he said, walking up to her.

She smiled. "Sure."

Andrew and Maria made their way through the crowd and started dancing and swaying to the music. He was not very good, at least that was his opinion. She was good. He felt good being with Maria, seeing her smile. He felt so relaxed with her. This would take his mind off of the weird stuff that had just happened. Some of the people made him laugh. It was good that they could let the stress of classes and lesson plans melt away for a moment by letting things loose. Some of the others were dancing crazily, almost inappropriately. He was happy for a few moments while he could forget about the strange man in the shadows.

Andrew drove Maria home from Russell's around midnight. As they drove, all he could think about was touching her hair and stroking the side of her cheek. He had had such a good time.

He walked Maria to the door of her apartment and he could hardly breathe. His hand was lightly on her elbow. She held her apartment key clasped in her hand.

Suddenly, Maria turned, stood on tip-toes and put her arms around him. The movement was graceful, but she took him by surprise.

"I have to find something out," she said.

She looked him in the eyes, moved closer, and tilted her head. He kissed her. A nervous kiss. Her tongue crept into a slow groove, moved so gracefully. She led, then switched gears and followed his savoring, pushed him closer, tighter to her a little at a time. He did the same and brought the curvature and firmness of the womanhood into focus, felt her breasts squeeze against his chest.

She opened her eyes, looked at him, and she smiled. Andrew was beginning to love that smile. She gently pulled away from him and he didn't want her to go.

She looked as delicate as a snowflake, and just as unique. In her eyes were friendship, and a twinkle of seriousness that made him shiver. Whenever her eyes met his, it felt like all of her attitude, all that crap that a woman picked up from struggling in a man's world, all of that dissipated.

Maria opened her apartment door and slowly backed inside. He didn't want her to go yet, but it was late. He was still overwhelmed by the kiss and he knew that she had a special effect on him. He would not be able to shake it.

"You're a good kisser," she said. "And I had a great time, Andrew."

"Thanks," he said. "And I can't wait for the sequel."

8

Everything had gone pretty well at dinner with Maria, so Andrew figured that everyone would leave him alone now. He didn't know what he would do next. He kept thinking about the way she kissed. How she tilted her head, eased her mouth open. The way she moved her tongue. Her voice. The way she moved. Maria was very nice but his schedule was crazy. Yet, he wondered about the man who was watching him from the shadows. His friend, Russell Kingston, came over to the lab to see him.

"Strange night, huh?" said Russell.

Andrew nodded. "It sure was."

"How was your date with Maria?"

"That was the only sane thing that happened last night," said Andrew. "She was okay."

Russell stared at him, nonplussed. "Okay? You're kidding, right?"

"Yeah," smiled Andrew, "just kidding. She was cool. I had a great time."

"You like her? I know she likes you."

Andrew knew his friend would say that. "We talked. We have a lot in common. She works as hard as I do and she's very pretty."

Russell smiled, and cocked his head. "So, you're going to see her again?"

"Yeah, why not?" said Andrew. "Thanks, buddy."

Russell heaved a sigh. "A gorgeous woman like that, and here you are, in your musty old lab, getting ready to do some crazy nonsense."

"It's not crazy," said Andrew. "It's work. You should try it sometime. Besides, we chose this path. We chose academia over an easy life. If we hadn't, we would be out on Nantucket Island partying it up."

"And meeting women."

"They may be drunk."

"At least you've met someone," said Russell.

"We're both pretty busy, but I'll catch up with her."

"Great. That's what I'm talking about," said Russell, looking at the cylinder, "What's that thing?"

Andrew looked over. "That's a project I'm working on."

"What is it?" said Russell. "Is this why you were being watched?"

"Maybe. I can't say anything about it yet."

"Oh," said Russell, coyly, "it's a secret."

"Yes."

"Well, if it's something not sanctioned by the college you know Doctor Winston could get you on this. He's crazy about private projects."

"If this thing works, I may have to ask you for your help."

Russell clasped his hands and smiled. "Partners in crime. I like it already," he said. "You know I have your back even though half the time I don't even know what you're talking about."

"Thanks, buddy, I knew I could count on you."

"Aren't you supposed to be working on a book about the school?"

"Yes, it's on-going."

"Just checking. That's not sanctioned by the college either, huh?"

"Nope."

"You know you can get yourself in some trouble. In fact, you could be too dangerous for me to be around."

"Since when have you been careful about stuff?"

He paused a moment. "You have a point there. You're one driven dude," said Russell. "I don't know if you're crazy or normal."

Andrew frowned. "Crazy is such a harsh word," he said.

"You're definitely not normal."

Andrew laughed. He liked it when Russell was around. He made him laugh. Maybe he wasn't normal, but he knew he wasn't crazy either. He hoped that he didn't end up killing himself over this project. Yet, if it worked, his life would change for the better.

9

Doctor Maria Salazar had to catch up on her classes. She was teaching a complementary wellness and restoration class and also a health assessment class. She was still thinking about her date with the great Doctor Andrew Thompson. It was a great and strange date all in one. It had started out well at the restaurant. She thought he looked very handsome and the conversation was great. Then after dinner as they were walking he thought he saw someone watching them. The party at Russell Kingston's apartment was great and then after that the kiss was fantastic. She thought that he liked her and had a great time too.

She led him back to her apartment, unsure whether she'd done the right thing. The truth was, she'd have liked to give herself to him. The guy looked great, and they liked each other. That should be enough. But she wasn't sure that she should encourage him. It was hard to see how any permanent relationship could evolve out of their circumstances. And she didn't want to hurt him for the sake of their own sexual pleasure.

It's the same way most women react to him. He's just there. Not unattractive, but nothing to make you look twice. But after a time after you get to know him, feel his quiet steadiness and strength, you wonder how you overlooked him. You remember how you weren't always on your best behavior around him. You begin to ask him questions about himself, like how he spends his time when he's not working.

She knew that he was always busy and she worried about him too. But seeing him out of his lab and classroom and in a different venue was great because she was able to see the real person. She didn't know if they could have any type of relationship. It would have been a unique one with their schedules but nothing was impossible.

She would see him walking around campus and thought he looked so handsome. But she also didn't think that she would be able to get very close to him. He never really opened up to anyone even though he had started doing it on the date. Would he talk to her? Would he trust her enough to dig underneath to who he was inside? The kiss was fantastic; he definitely was a great kisser. She would have to see how it went.

Talking about her mother during dinner brought back some tough memories. There was something to the question of "If you could go back in time and change something, what would it be?" Yet, that was the question, and she thought about her mother and why she never had gotten any help for her cancer. Her mother would say, "Maria, don't worry about me, I'll be okay." But she still died. Maybe that was why she went into nursing.

She also wondered about Andrew's project. Was he in any trouble? Why would someone be watching him? Was it the police? Was he doing something illegal in the lab? She made her way down through the Center for Theoretical Physics near his lab and he walked out the door. She stopped and looked at him. He smiled warmly.

"Hi, Maria."

She felt her heart pound in her chest. "Andrew, it's good to see you."

He nodded. "I had a great time last night. We were up late."

"Yes, we were but I had a great time too. As I said, you are a great kisser."

Andrew fidgeted a moment, and then said, "Are you free for lunch?"

"Yeah, I have my health assessment class in a few. I could meet you afterwards."

"That would be great," he smiled. "I can't wait."

"Okay," she smiled in anticipation, "I better get going. I'll see you."

"Sure."

They parted and Maria continued through the crowd down the hall in the opposite direction. She turned around and saw him standing there watching her go. She smiled. Maybe he was a little shy. He didn't go out with people too much. He did like her and maybe there was something to the kiss and the evening. He couldn't wait to see her. She would see where this would go.

Later, in the cafeteria, they met and sat down at a table. He frowned, and seemed distracted. She wondered by his expression if something was wrong. Did she do something wrong? Did she say something wrong? What happened?

"Anything wrong, Andrew?"

He shook his head. "No, I'm just tired," he smiled, shyly. "I really enjoyed myself last night, Maria. I've always wanted to talk to you but I never got up the nerve to do it."

She nodded encouragingly and smiled. Yes, he was definitely shy, but adorable. "You can always talk to me, Andrew. I don't mind."

"Thank you, I really would like that."

It was a pleasant time. Andrew talked about his home life and his dreams. There was something guarded about him though. There was something that he was holding back on. She didn't want to push it. She was just happy that he was talking to her. Maybe as time went on, he would open up more.

"There's something I have to do," he said, suddenly gravely. "It's something really big. I just wanted to see you and talk to you before I did it."

She stared wide-eyed at him. "Is it a secret?"

"Yes."

"Your special project?"

"Yes. I can't tell you what it is yet, but if it works it could change everything."

"Change everything?"

He nodded. "Everything."

She smiled with anticipation. Whenever anyone said something could change "everything," it usually was something big. She just hoped it was something good. "I can't wait to hear what it is."

"I can't wait to tell you," he said, smiling shyly.

Maria was so happy that Andrew had told her this. There was something that was important to him that he wanted to share with her. Yet she wondered if it was dangerous. Was it life threatening? Did he think this would be the last time he would talk with her?

10

Andrew needed to test the machine. He had been working on it for so long and now was the time. He had tinkered with it trying to get everything right. But he needed to test it to see if it would actually work. It was no good running the simulations and not knowing if it would stick. He needed to do a field test. He didn't have any animals to test his theory. He had not thought to do that. He would have to send himself.

And what about air? Would he be able to breathe in there for long? A human could last for hours on a proportional amount. Only hours. He would need some water and maybe even food. In fact, he could do the experiment without any of that, assuming it would only take minutes. If the minutes did drag into hours, he could abort it and return.

Why not go back to the year1888 and see if it worked and also if he could make contact with the girl? It would be a first both ways. He didn't even think of the danger. He would program the time and place. Jennie would monitor his progress. What could go wrong? If his calculations were correct, he knew that Rowena Michaels would probably be in the dorm for study period. He hoped he had studied the right bulletin to know where and when the classes were. But if he went in the evening, he didn't know whether they went to bed when the sun went down. But he could get in and get out and get back to make the notes about the trip. If he could make contact with her, it would bridge the time gap, like Sean had said. He could cross over into something wonderful. He pressed the button on the control panel and the lights flickered.

It would be get in and get out. And, of course, try not to get killed in the process.

"Jennie," he said, nervously. His heart was pounding. "Is the ship ready to jump?"

"Affirmative," said the female voice. "Coordinates set in and entering the vortex now."

Andrew pulled the lever and held tightly onto the console. It jumped a bit but was not bad. There was a creaking sound as it felt like the machine was being pushed forward. He hoped it was not going to break up on him. His sweaty hands gripped the console. He thought he was going to die. He prayed that he had not jumped too soon.

When the shaking stopped and the noise ended, Andrew realized it was over and he let out a sigh of relief. The ship was still intact and he was still breathing. Hopefully he was not still in his lab. That would have been such a letdown.

"Jennie, where am I? When is it?"

"Time date: March 28, 1888."

Andrew shivered. "What?" he said. "I made it?"

"Affirmative."

Andrew thought he was going to leap out of his skin. This was amazing. He had crossed over the bridge and moved into a new dimension. He shivered just thinking about it. This could answer so many questions especially the ones that his students had raised and also some of his own. Now he was going to walk into a whole new world.

"It's show time," he said, putting on a communication bracelet. "Secure the ship, Jennie. I'm going out to take a look."

"Confirmed."

He sighed and clicked off the engine. Picking up a black leather duster, he brushed it off and put it on. He also grabbed his black fedora and opened the door.

He closed his eyes and slowly stepped outside the door and took a deep breath of 19th century air. He opened his eyes and saw the old Victorian building in its 19th century incarnation. He shivered as he looked at the building with its porch wrapping around, the stairs going up to the door and the bell tower on top. It looked lonely all by itself. The other buildings had not been built yet. He looked back at the time ship and saw that it had blended with its surroundings and became an oak tree. He realized that no one had noticed his arrival. Everything had gone well.

Andrew touched his wrist communicator. "Everything's well here, Jennie," he said. "I do not feel any after effects of the trip and the air smells and feels great."

"Affirmative," she said.

"Keep monitoring the operating systems and get the ship ready for the return trip. I won't be long."

"Understood," she said.

He had arrived in late March when it was dark and a bit chilly. He was happy there was no snow on the ground, even for New England. He was also happy for the coat he wore even though it was a modern overcoat.

He had memorized the map of the campus in 1888. He knew where the buildings were. He walked off to his right and saw the two white dormitories, East Hall and West Hall, which looked bigger than he had expected. But then he realized he may have made a mistake. He should have thought this whole thing out a bit.

"What was I thinking?" he shivered. "Now I'm a black man in the nineteenth century. I should have thought this through a little more."

Would he be able to walk in the front door or be told to go around to the back? He had not thought about that. He walked toward the girls' dorm which was East Hall, thinking of what he could do. He wondered if security would see him wandering around. He didn't want to be locked up in a nineteenth century jail.

Andrew slowly walked up to the girls' dorm's front door and knocked. He didn't know what would happen. Would they even open the door? When they saw him standing there, would they even let him inside? It wasn't the south but there was still plenty of prejudice and racism at this time in history. Would Rowena even come down to see him? He had all these thoughts going through his mind as he waited for a response.

A young freckled faced blonde woman, who may have been 17 or 18 years old, opened the door, dressed in the 19th century dress, and he almost lost his voice and his nerve. He was finally going to interact with someone from the past. What would his students say to him now? She stared up at him. "May I help you?" she said.

He bowed and removed his hat, respectfully. "Good evening, miss, I am here to speak with Miss Rowena Michaels," he said. "I have a message for her. It won't take long."

Surprisingly, the young woman nodded and opened the door so he could step into the lobby of the dorm. He edged through the door slowly, then stopped halfway, before stepping through. He saw that the lobby was lit with kerosene lamps and couches and chairs were spread throughout. The girls were calling Rowena to the lobby. Would she come?

He had not expected anything like this; he had not thought that this world would be so utterly different from his own that it would intimidate him. On the smooth walls were several paintings of nature scenes. He would have wanted to examine them, but dared not. Then he listened; he felt very uncomfortable.

Andrew hung onto his hat tightly as he walked over by the stairs where he could see her when she came down. He could feel all their eyes on him and suddenly he felt the temperature of the room increase. There were two young men dressed in nineteenth century suit and tie, who had come to visit their ladies watching him. He hoped there would not be a confrontation. They almost went cross-eyed at the sight of him. West Hall, the boys' dorm, was right next door. He sat in a chair to ward off his nervousness. His heart was pounding and he was almost feeling lightheaded. His right leg was jumping a little from his nervousness. He tried to take deep breaths to calm himself. He was more nervous now than he was on his date with Maria. What would he say to Rowena?

It didn't take long before Miss Michaels came slowly down the stairs. She wore a very nice velvet 19th century style dress with the long sleeves and high neck. It almost looked scary seeing all these women in these dresses. When he was doing his research he saw the dresses on headless mannequins which gave him the chills. While she was coming down the stairs, Andrew stood. She wore a confused look on her face. She was a petite woman with skin like vanilla cinnamon and dark hair arranged in a bun. In fact, all the women he saw in the lobby had ivory skin and confused looks on their faces. He needed to do this, and make it quick. These people were New Englanders and the sun didn't shine so much at this time of the year. He had to get past his nervousness and get the job done. He saw that he was looking at the actual breathing person from the photograph.

Andrew cleared his throat as she reached the bottom step. "Miss Michaels, may I talk to you for a moment?" he said. "I have a message for you."

She looked at him, blankly, as if studying his intent, and then moved slowly to the back of the large room. Andrew knew he had to make this quick because he was very uncomfortable. The two young men stood and were staring at him. This was not going to turn out right if he took too long. She sat down stiffly on the very edge of the couch, knees together, beautiful hands clasped on her lap, looking up at him. He just lightly sat on the other side of the couch.

"Miss Michaels, my name is Doctor Andrew Thompson. I have come many millions of miles to see you," he said, reaching into his pocket. "There is something I need to show you."

He pulled out the picture and handed it to her. She took it gingerly and her eyes widened when she looked at it. "I was researching the history of the school," he said, "and I saw this picture in the book. I made a copy of it. Do you know what it is?"

She was staring at the picture and then she looked at him. "This is my graduation picture with the other girls from my class. We just took it today. I'm seated at the right," she said, shaking her head. "But how did you get this? In a book?"

"Yes, Miss Michaels, as I said I was researching the history of our school. I was a student here or at least I will be," he said, thinking of what he had just said. He was not used to talking like this. "You can show the picture to the other girls. I had found some information on you but not very much. I had to come meet you. I'm going to have to leave now and go back to my ship. I have one other thing for you."

He stood and put his hand in his coat pocket again and pulled out a coin. He held it up in front of him. "This is not worth anything now, but it soon will be," he said, as he took her pale hand and placed the coin in it and closed it. "When you get back to your room, look at the date on the coin and then you'll understand. Goodbye, Miss Rowena. If all goes well, maybe I'll be able to come back to see you."

He bowed slightly to her and turned and walked to the door. "Ladies and gentlemen," he said, slightly bowing as he opened the door and stepped outside into the night.

He put his hat on and rushed down the stairs where he was met by four young white men. They walked up to him with angry looks on their faces. Andrew didn't know what to expect. He just knew he was in trouble.

"Hey," said one of them as they surrounded him. "Who are you and what are you doing here?"

Andrew gulped. This was not good. "I just came to deliver a message," he said.

"We don't want any trouble," said a voice behind him.

"No trouble here, I'm heading out and you don't have to worry about a thing."

Andrew kept thinking that they were going to beat him up. While he was speaking with Rowena one of the other boys in the lobby must have run over to the boys' dorm to let them know he was there. There was only one way he could get out of this one. He put his communicator to his lips and pressed the button. "Jennie, prepare for launch. Teleport me to the ship."

Immediately there was a ray of light around him and he was suddenly standing on a trans mat pad in the control room of the time ship. He felt his chest, his head, his arms and legs to make sure everything was still there. The teleport had worked. Thank goodness for small favors. He knew that it had probably scared the living daylights out of those boys. At this point he didn't care. He just knew that it was time to go home.

The ship hummed quietly as it made its way back to the present. Andrew's heart raced as he thought of his experience in the girls' dorm in 1888. He took a deep breath. He couldn't stop thinking about it. He had really been there. He had really interacted with real people from another century. This was unbelievable.

The lights stopped blinking and the ship had come to a stop. He took a deep breath and opened the door. He stumbled out the door back into his lab. It was dark. He had returned to the campus at night.

He had to make notes about his experience before he forgot. He turned on the light and stumbled over to his desk. He took off his wrist communicator. He felt so dizzy, so disorientated. What was wrong with him? Was it because of the dimensional vortex? Was it time sickness? Was he experiencing time lag, like jet lag always was? This was a strange feeling. He took a deep breath and fell into his chair.

"Jennie," he said, "is everything functioning properly with the time ship?"

"Affirmative," said the computer's voice, echoing in the lab. "All system's fully functioning."

"Any abnormalities, any detection of viruses?"

"Negative. No abnormalities or viruses detected."

He shook his head. "Why do I feel this way? I feel so weak, so tired."

"Suggest diagnostic on cabin air pressure."

"Begin diagnostic immediately, Jennie. Everything worked out well. First test flight successful."

It would have been like being concerned every time he got home for the night and opened the door, wondering what might be inside. Certainly there was the chance of a surprise, but not the sort of surprise that might threaten not only him but also all he cared about.

What if something dangerous slipped in from a different dimension?

He thought about Rowena. She looked just like her picture. Did he expect her to look any different than the picture? Wow! It was the exact day her picture was taken. Amazing! It was good to meet her, even though it was a little scary. Walking into that dorm lobby, with the women looking at him, was a bit uncomfortable. He had expected a confrontation with the two young men who were there. But the four men on the outside could have done serious damage to him in a big way. He had gone into a primitive and hostile environment and was happy that he had the teleport. He had not anticipated that, but at least, he didn't get in any trouble, at least, not yet.

Ever since boyhood, Andrew had sensed a presence guiding him, a force that was always there, constantly directing his actions. He often felt it viscerally, and was convinced that it told him whether or not he was doing the right thing. His stomach was calm now, but the sensation didn't always provide him with consistent indicators. It seemed to have lapses ... unpredictable and disconcerting gaps.

He was lucky tonight. The whole thing with the boys at the dorm could have gone badly.

He turned on his computer and began transcribing his notes about the trip. He recorded his sensations, perceptions, overviews, and opinions about the people, especially Rowena Michaels. She was the reason he had gone there in the first place. Jennie would record all trips made in the time ship. This one had been successful. Now he could move forward and do even more. He looked belatedly at the clock. It read 10:06:22. The ship had only officially been gone for ten minutes, in its own frame of reference. The diagnostic check would improve functions or conditions inside the ship. He could not afford to get any type of sickness. He was not going to bring any type of plague to his own time.

Andrew wondered what Rowena thought about him. How often do you have a strange black man appearing out of nowhere with a picture of you from a book? A picture that you just took that day? Would she check out the coin? Would she understand? Would he ever see her again?

Forgetting about the calculations and notes, he analyzed his growing attraction to Rowena as if it were an experiment, but he couldn't fit his emotions into a suitable framework. And it had happened quickly. Was he falling in love with a historical figure? This was getting interesting.

Then the screen lit up and the ringer went off startling him back to the present. It was Maria.

He answered it. "Hello?"

The screen changed to the smiling Maria Salazar. She was apparently at home in her apartment. He could feel a smile coming across his face as he looked at her. "Hi Andrew," she said, and then she frowned. "Oh, I'm sorry, you're still working in your lab. Did I interrupt something?"

"No, Maria, I was just finishing up. I was doing a test and it was successful."

"That's great. Was this the one you were talking about?"

"Yes it was. It was successful. I just have to make a couple of adjustments but it worked out well."

"Can you talk about it yet?"

Andrew frowned. "Not yet, Maria. Still more tests to do before I reveal it."

"Did you want to come over tonight?"

Andrew thought a moment and then sighed. From all that was on his mind, Maria brought a smile to his lips. He didn't think he should go over to Maria that evening. He was definitely tired and he still had Rowena Michaels on his mind. Now he had two women on his mind. He wanted to share this with Maria but it was too soon. She wouldn't understand. "I'm going to have to take a raincheck, Maria. Maybe this weekend we could get together."

"Sure," she said, "that would be great. Have a great night, Andrew."

"You too, Maria. Take care," he said, as the link disconnected.

Andrew yawned and decided that was it for the day and closed up the lab. He had some papers to grade for his classes. He had to remember he was still a professor with a job to do. This had definitely been a good day. He was so excited he didn't know what to do. Would he be able to sleep? Would he be able to work? What would his students say about time travel if they knew he had done it? When would he try it again? He knew he would dream about Rowena.

Wait a minute! Why was he always thinking so much about Rowena? Was it because she was from the past? He had Maria. First, he had no women; now he had two, one from the past and one from the present. This was crazy.

For the first time in his life he had a purpose for pushing on this time and it was about seeing Rowena again.

11

Rowena spoke with the other three girls in her graduating class in her room, Sadie Graham who was her roommate, Sarah Bell, and Carla Snow. She never thought she would have a meeting like this. When she received the call from the desk she thought something had happened at home with her parents. She never expected this. When she saw him, she hesitated a bit. She'd never seen a black person before, and she was fascinated by the man's skin. The girls had heard about the mysterious black man who had come to see her. They looked at the picture Andrew had handed to Rowena and shook their heads.

"Is this real?" said Sarah Bell, waving her dark hair.

"Did that man really give you this?" said Carla Snow, with her large hazel eyes. Her hair, brilliant blonde and brown, curled around her face.

"Where did he get this from?" said Sadie Graham, shaking her head. She had short dark hair tied behind in a loose bun. Her calm brown eyes looked straight ahead. Generous lips, normally relaxed with poised determination.

"He said he got it out of a book of the school's history he was researching," said Rowena.

"Who is he?" said Sadie. "What book could he had gotten this from? We just took the picture today."

Rowena nodded. "I know it was most strange."

"He even touched you?" said Sarah.

"Yes," said Rowena. "He took my hand and placed the coin in it."

Sarah scowled. "That is not right," she said. "How dare he?"

"He said his name is Doctor Andrew Thompson. He's an historian," said Rowena.

"Where did he come from?" said Sarah. "We don't have any colored teachers here."

"I don't think he's from around here," said Rowena. She thought about his words, the way he phrased them. They were unusual. It was like he was from the future. "It was very strange. The way he talked it was like he was from another time. He's the man from beyond tomorrow."

Other girls came by the room when they heard about what had happened. There was so much excitement in the air that the ladies' dean, Mrs. Knowles, her grayish hair tied up in a bun, came by to see what was happening.

"What is going on here?" she said, standing in the doorway, hands on hips, her piercing blue eyes shone accusingly.

"Mrs. Knowles, we were just looking at the picture that the man gave me downstairs," said Rowena.

"I heard about that," she said, frowning. "Very strange. I'm going to have to speak with Principal Bell about this. We can't have strange colored men coming to the dorm so late in the evening. Please ladies, keep it down."

"Yes, ma'am," said Carla, as the headmistress walked off.

"He gave me something else," Rowena said, looking around the room. "Where did I put it? Where is that coin?"

"The coin he handed to you?" said Carla.

"Yes," Rowena said, grabbing the coin. "Sadie, where's your magnifying glass?"

"It's over here," said Sadie, picking up the magnifying glass from the small desk. "What is that?"

"The coin he gave me," said Rowena, taking the magnifying glass. "He said to take a look at the date."

Rowena searched for the date on the coin. It was a very strange piece; it looked like silver. It was a quarter dollar and she recognized the picture of George Washington on it. It also said United States of America. She turned the coin around and around searching before she saw the date. She shivered when she read what it said.

"What is it, Rowena?" said Sarah.

"I found the date," she said.

"What does it say?" said Sadie.

"2022," she said. "It says the year of the coin is 2022. He had said the coin was not worth anything now but soon would be."

"Wait a minute," said Sadie. "Rowena, are you saying that the colored man is from the future?"

"From the words he said to me," said Rowena, "it's very possible. His clothes were different. The way he talked was different too. And then he just disappeared."

"He disappeared?" said Carla.

"Yes," said Rowena, putting the coin on the dresser. "Some boys were waiting for him outside the door and surrounded him. They said he just disappeared. There was a light that surrounded him and he vanished."

"That is so strange," said Sadie.

"That is weird," said Sarah.

"Wow!" said Carla. "Could he had been an angel?"

Sarah grunted. "A colored angel?"

"Well," said Carla, "they could come in different colors."

"Whatever it is," said Rowena, "it was strange. It wasn't a dream because he left behind two things."

"I still can't get over the picture, Rowena," said Sadie, looking at it. "We just took the picture today. How did he get it? Does he know Mr. Wallace?"

"I don't think that's the answer," said Rowena. "And unless he comes back, I guess we'll never know."

Rowena didn't know what to make of this strange doctor. Did this man say he would return to see her? What was it about her that she was singled out? He had said he would return if all worked out. Where did he come from? People would definitely know when he came back. She knew her father had done some work after the Civil War with former slaves. She shook her head. She would have to wait and see what happened next.

12

Things began to calm down after a time but Rowena still had the incident with the strange doctor in her mind. As she and Sadie got ready for bed, she didn't think that she would ever forget about this night. She changed into her long white nightgown and washed her face with water from the basin on the dry sink.

She noticed that Sadie was shaken about this too. The other girls were very crazy about it too. The report from the boys about his disappearance made them a little on edge and a little excited. Rowena would need to take the picture to Mr. Wallace to have him take a long look at it and she would need to probably have Principal Bell take a look at the coin too.

Yet, if the man had disappeared it had to mean that he was from the future. What would make a person disappear like that? The boys had surrounded him. Everything about him was strange, his words, his clothes, his mannerisms. He had even touched her. Surely, no Negro man would do that to a respected white woman.

"Are you okay, Rowena?" said Sadie, walking over to her.

"Yes, Sadie," she smiled, taking a deep breath, "I'm fine. I guess we better get to bed before Mrs. Knowles has something to say about it."

Sadie stared at her, concern etched on the corners of her eyes. "It's about that colored man. Did he do something to you? Did he hurt you?"

"No, he didn't. I was just thinking about his words."

"You still think he was from the future?"

"So many strange things happened. What else could it be? Some supernatural disturbance?"

Sadie sighed. "I don't know," she said. "It was strange. Do you think he'll come back?"

"I don't know. It may be nice to see him again to get some answers."

Sadie gasped. "You want to see him again?"

Rowena nodded. "Just to get answers. Why would he come with a picture of us that we just took and say it came from a book? Why would he single me out? Why was he dressed like that?"

"He even touched you and got away with it."

Rowena kept thinking about his words. "Sadie, I believe Doctor Thompson is from the future. He said he was a student here or at least he would be. He said he came a million miles to see me. The words he used show he is from another time."

"A Negro doctor from the future?" said Sadie, shaking her head. "A nigger doctor? I don't know about that. This may not be the South, but who would go to see him? It sounds like a strange new world."

Rowena considered her roommate's words. It would be an interesting world all right. She had always heard that Negroes could not learn and were not that smart even though schools were being built for them. If he was from the future that meant that black people were smart and could learn. What was he a doctor of? She secretly wished he would come back.

13

Andrew returned to the year 1888 not just to visit Rowena but to play baseball with the boys. He knew it would be good to see her and he knew she would be told he was there. It had been three weeks by their time since he had last been there. It had only been a few days for him. He wondered if they had missed him or even remembered him. Andrew had no idea what his initial visit to Rowena had done through the campus. What was said? If you go back and interact or change anything that happened before, it could change the future. That remained to be seen. He had researched that the boys would play baseball in a field near the boys' dorm in the springtime. He loved baseball and wished he could play it in his time but the sport had gone bankrupt after it had once been America's favorite pastime.

He ran over to where the field was. The boys were organizing themselves for a game. He hoped there was room for him to play as well. The boys looked at him strangely not knowing who he was. Andrew realized that he had just appeared out of nowhere. He was just passing through. He wondered if he would be able to function in the past as he did in the present, running and jumping around.

"Hey guys, can I play baseball with you?" he said, running up to them. He saw they were wearing light colored baseball uniforms from the period with collared tops, buttoned in the front. They wore small caps and dark pants with a white belt. White socks came up to the knees.

"Where did you come from?" said a brown-haired kid.

"Over there," Andrew said, pointing behind him.

The boys looked past him and saw a tree. They shook their heads.

"I have my glove," he said, holding it up. It was an old glove but still more modern than theirs.

"Wait a minute," said a dark-haired kid, "you're the one who came to the girls' dorm back a few weeks ago. You talked with Rowena Michaels and then disappeared."

Andrew shivered. He remembered the confrontation he had with the boys outside the dorm. "Yeah, that was me," he said, feeling his heart pound. "Well, what do you say? Can I play?"

One of the men there, who was probably a teacher, stepped up. He had a full dark beard, looked to be in great shape. It was a very impressive beard. "What position do you play?" he said.

"I could be a catcher. I have a catcher's mask."

The man took the mask and examined it. He shook his head. "Never seen anything like this before," he said. "Did you make it?"

"No," said Andrew. "It just came into my procession."

Andrew had put on his pinstripe pants like the Yankees used to wear. He knew it looked unusual since the Yankees were not around yet. He also had the dark blue Yankee cap with the white interlocking NY on it. He wore a dark blue tee-shirt. There were a couple of men playing. They were probably teachers. He noticed that they wore their beards well. Beards were a big thing at this period of time. Very fashionable. He knew that black people did play at this time but soon would be banned from playing with white people.

They organized into teams. Andrew found himself catching and began warming up the boy, named Gus, who was pitching. Gus would go into a full windup to throw the ball. He would swing his arms above his head a couple of times and then deliver the ball. It came in with some speed but not much. The game didn't look much different. They played in different clothes that looked like it was from a different period of time which he had to remember he was in now. He remembered seeing pictures of the Cincinnati Redlegs of the 1870s who would beat everyone they played. This would have been the period they would have played. The National League had been organized in 1876.

Andrew was happy he was able to hit the ball well and run. The other boys and teachers were impressed with him. He quickly was able to learn their names and win their trust. He knew they would wonder where he had come from. Why he was so different? Who he really was. He knew it would be hard to explain. "Yeah, guys, I'm from the future." He would be locked up in a cell so far underground, he would be a living time capsule because no one would ever see him again. Did they have asylums around there?

He came up to the plate to bat. The bat itself felt so light in his hands. It was probably a homemade broom made in the broom shop in the basement of Founders' Hall. He took a swing at a pitch and lined it down the right field line. Taking off he rounded the bases and slid into third base with a triple. He stood up and dusted himself off. Jackie Robinson eat your heart out. He liked Josh Gibson better though. He was a great catcher and slugger. Boy it felt good running. He could do this all day.

14

Doctor Robert Winston sat at his desk looking over the reports from his professors. He wished there was something more he could do. But he was living a good life. Framed photos of his wife, Roxanne, and their two boys, Shawn, ten, and Derek, eleven, smiled back at him on his desk. He was a tall black man with salt and pepper hair and plenty of experience handling professors who thought they knew everything. If he could get a little more respect from Andrew Thompson, everything would be great. The young man was brilliant, too brilliant for his own good. So what if he had a degree in astrophysics. Thompson was an example of the new wave of professors who thought they knew everything. Maybe the guy should go into space.

"Doctor Winston," said Marsha on the intercom.

"Yes, Marsha?"

"There's a Mr. Smith here from the National Security Department to see you."

"Really? Show him in."

Winston wondered if he was in any trouble. Why would National Security be coming to the college? It was definitely a mystery. Did he do anything that he had forgotten about? Was there a project of his under investigation? He couldn't think of anything he had done to warrant a visit from a representative of National Security. He was almost nervous.

The man walked in. He looked to be six feet tall with blond hair and a black suit, white shirt and red tie. He smiled and came toward Winston's enormous desk.

"Doctor Robert Winston?"

"Yes," said Winston, standing.

"I am Hank Smith, National Security Department," he said, extending his hand.

Winston took it. "Good to meet you, Mr. Smith," he said, shaking the man's hand. "Have a seat."

Smith took his seat across from the desk. He smiled and looked straight at Winston. "I guess you're wondering why I'm here."

"It did cross my mind," said Winston, settling back into his chair.

"Well, I won't take up too much of your time, but we have been watching one of your professors very carefully."

"Oh, who is that?"

"Doctor Andrew Thompson."

Winston almost fell out of his chair. "Really?" he said, palms down on the desk. "What could he have done to endanger national security?"

"Doctor Thompson is doing something very interesting in his lab."

"What is he doing?"

"It has something to do with time."

"Time?"

"Yes, it could even be a time machine."

Winston leaned back in his chair and stared at Smith. "And who is it that you work for?" he said. "Government?"

"I work for an organization that handles national security. We believe that Doctor Thompson is in possession of something that could be harmful to our country's security. You can understand, Doctor Winston, the way things have been lately how we could be concerned."

"A time machine?" Winston still couldn't believe it.

"Yes."

"But that's impossible," said Winston. "Time travel is impossible."

Smith smiled. "Not for your Doctor Thompson," he said. "He has crossed the bridge."

"What?" said Winston, "The bridge?"

"Yes," said Smith, "the bridge of time. He has made two trips to the past."

Winston stood quickly and began to pace back and forth. "Time travel?" he said, thinking, and then he looked at Smith. "By the way, how do you know this?"

"Remember I've been watching him. He's seen me. You should see what he's doing in his lab. That's where the answers are."

"In the lab?"

"Yes sir. It's in the lab."

Winston considered it for a moment and shook his head. It was incredible. "Thank you for the information," he said, standing.

Smith stood and smiled. "Thank you for your time, sir," he said, shaking Winston's hand. "Keep your eye on Thompson, we surely will."

Winston shook his hand. "Thank you. We will definitely keep an eye on him too."

Smith walked out and Winston smiled. Now Thompson had gone too far. A time machine? Winston thought about what he could do with that. He smiled. If he could get his hands on it, the sky would be the limit. Could it be possible?

A man walked out from a room in the back. He was about six feet tall, dark hair and wore a gray uniform. He walked around the back of the desk and stood at near attention in front of Winston, who looked at him and frowned.

"Did you hear that?" said Winston, solemnly.

"Yes sir, very interesting."

"Thompson's intelligent, but he is also ambitious and envious and wants to stay out of trouble." Winston rolled a pen between his fingers. "We have to be careful."

"Yes sir."

"Mr. Walker, I want you to go to Thompson's lab and see what he has in there that would have National Security up in arms."

Walker sat down calmly in the chair in front of Winston's desk. "You may want to cut the college's connection to him."

Winston blinked. "What?" he said. "Cut the connection ...?"

"Fire him. Get him off the payroll. If National Security sees him as some kind of threat, he needs to be eliminated."

"Maybe, but I can't just fire him."

"Why not?" said Walker. "You should talk it over with the board. I could snoop around the lab even though I don't think Thompson would like that."

"True," said Winston, sitting down. "You're going to have to do it after dark. Do it after he's gone."

"Is that ethical?"

"This is important. Thompson may be hiding something and we need to know what it is."

"Yes sir. When do you want me to do it?"

Winston stared Walker intently in the eye. "As soon as you can," he said. "Get in, look around, and get out. Looks like the whiz kid's days are numbered."

15

Rowena was in the library studying hard for her examinations. She just had to finish with her English literature and mathematics. Even as she studied she couldn't help but think about Andrew Thompson. It was such a mystery that he just showed up one day with her graduation picture and the coin. To think that he came all the way from the future to see her was unbelievable. She would study hard. He said he would try to return. But that was three weeks ago. He said he would try to return if he could. Was he in trouble? Did something happen to him because of his trip? She wanted him to return. But then it would seem a little weird to be walking and talking with him. Was life between the races different in the future?

Sarah came rushing in looking excited. Miss Stoneham, the elderly librarian, frowned at Sarah for making such noise. What was the commotion all about?

Sarah sat down across from her, smiling and catching her breath. Rowena looked at her friend, curiously. "You look like you're about to burst," she whispered. "What's going on?"

"Rowena," she said, "He's back. The colored man's back from the future."

Some of the other students at a nearby table turned and looked at them. A dark-haired boy named Roger looked at Rowena. "You were with that traveler, the Negro man?" he said.

Rowena turned to him. "Yes, he came to see me three weeks ago."

The two girls at the other table looked at Rowena in astonishment. A brown-haired girl grew pale as if she'd seen the sun. "You mean that was true?" she said.

"Yes, I'm afraid so," said Sarah. "Rowena has a Negro man coming after her."

Rowena stared over at her friend and frowned. "I do not, Sarah. Stop that."

"Jeff and Robert were over at East Hall that night when he came in to talk to you," said Roger. "Jeff told some of the other boys and they surrounded him when he came out but he disappeared right in front of them."

Rowena remembered that and wondered if everything was okay with him. Where had he gone to? Was he really an angel like Carla said? How did he disappear? There were so many questions. She started getting very excited just thinking about it.

Rowena stared at Sarah for a moment and blinked hard. She could hardly believe it. "Doctor Andrew?" she said, jumping out of her chair. Now Miss Stoneham was frowning at Rowena.

"He's playing baseball with the boys down at the field," smiled Sarah. "I couldn't believe it either, but it's him. No doubt about it. He's back. Could he be from the future?"

Rowena stood and gathered her books quickly. She hurried out the library followed by Sarah and a few other students. She had forgotten about her studies and wanted to get over to him as quickly as possible. What did this all mean? They hurried over to the field where the boys were finishing up their game. She was wearing a long sleeve and long necked white dress but she sat on the bleacher seat and watched the game. Rowena didn't know where he was at first. She searched around the entire field. Sarah pointed him out behind the batter catching Gus who was pitching. She was impressed at how well he played. He was wearing pinstripe pants and a mask over his face. Could they be from the future?

When Andrew looked over and saw her watching the game, he smiled that signature smile. He did look handsome for a Negro. Was she beginning to like him? Was that even possible? Why would he come back in time just to play baseball?

16

After the game, everyone stood around talking. Andrew was impressed at how well they played. The game had not changed much. He had read that the game started simply. It was played in many different ways. The variations of the game depended on the region of the country. The Massachusetts Plan, the New York Plan, and the fields in Hoboken, New Jersey. It had been a good game. He had fun. He was glad he had come here to play. He was happy with his performance. The two teachers had left apparently to attend to some business. They stared at him as they left. He knew he impressed them by his play but they still didn't know who he was. He needed to make sure he didn't stay long.

Rowena looked great dressed in white. He was so happy she had come. He knew it wouldn't take long for someone to tell her he was there.

"It's good to see you, Rowena," he said, smiling.

"You play the game well," she said. "You've played baseball before?"

He smiled, "I don't get a chance to play very much anymore," he said, "but I'm happy I was able to play today."

Rowena smiled at him. He remembered that she was just eighteen years old and from a different era. There was so much that he wanted to ask her but in front of all her friends and schoolmates it was not the time. He would have to wait for that.

"I never noticed that tree over there," said Charles, a redhead, looking off in the distance. "Where did that come from?"

He had a feeling this might happen. "That's no tree," said Andrew, shaking his head. "That's my ship. You want to look inside?"

"Inside a tree?" said Sarah.

Andrew smiled. "You'll be surprised by what could be inside a tree."

He was hesitant about showing the ship, but it had been noticed. He guessed that someone would eventually notice a tree, especially an oak tree that was not there before. He just didn't think it would be noticed so quickly. The last time he had come it was dark and everyone had been in for study time or bedtime so it was not noticed. He figured there was nothing much he could do about that.

"Okay," said Andrew, "you can look inside, but only for a moment."

There were 12 of them, which was a lot. They marched over to the tree. He took out his key, found the keyhole and turned. The students shook their heads. He knew it looked crazy. This was his ship? When the door opened and they looked inside the door, their mouths dropped.

"By the way," he said, "did I mention, it's bigger on the inside than the outside."

He stepped in and the students slowly and cautiously moved through the door of the living ship. Their eyes bulged and they gawked at the technology of the machine.

"Welcome to my time ship," he said, putting his glove and mask down inside the door. "Don't touch anything."

"How big is it?" said Harry, a short, dark-haired boy.

"It's pretty big. It took me about eight years to build. I did it around my studies to become a doctor."

"Does everyone in the future have a time ship?" said Charles.

"No, I may have the only one. I tested it when I first came here."

"You mean you used this back in March when you came to see Rowena?" said Roger.

"That's right."

Gus was about to touch one of the controls on the panel, and Andrew slapped his hand. Gus flinched. "Dude, I said, no touching," he said, thinking that Sean used to say that being the California dude he was.

"Can anyone run this ship?" said Roger.

"No," said Andrew, "I am the only one that can operate it. It's attuned to my DNA."

They looked confused. "What's DNA?" said Sarah.

"It's in most of the cells in our bodies. I'll explain. It's like fingerprints; everybody has a unique pattern." He smiled, looking over the controls. "This ship is attuned to my DNA."

The ship was not really attuned to his DNA. He figured trying to explain everything would fry their brains. So he left it there.

Sarah shook her head. "Where in the future are you from?"

Andrew didn't expect all the questions but he was not surprised by them. He had to end this thing. He didn't want to attract too much attention even though it may have gone too far already. He didn't want the teachers coming back and wondering where all their students were. Did he kidnap part of the student body?

"I'm from the far future," he said.

"The man from beyond tomorrow," said Rowena.

Andrew looked at her. This was the first time he had seen her since that evening in the dorm and had tried to explain. She understood now.

"Yes," he smiled, "that's right. I like that. The man from beyond tomorrow."

"Can we go with you to the future?" said Jack, a tall dark-haired boy, almost jumping up and down with excitement.

Andrew saw him and frowned. "No, you're not going," he said. "Everyone out. Tour is over. Out, except for Rowena. Watch your step on the way out. Thanks for coming."

Andrew went over to the door and let them out. They filed out even though they did so reluctantly. A couple of the boys hesitated because they saw that Rowena would be alone with Andrew but he brushed them out the door.

When they were all gone and Andrew closed the door, he went back up to the control panel where Rowena stood. She was pensive, standing there looking beautiful in her nineteenth century long sleeved, high necked white dress.

"What do you think about this, Ro?"

She looked at him as if studying his face and searching for the words.

"I don't know what to say," she said, softly. "You were telling the truth. You're really from the future."

"Yes, I was telling the truth. You looked at the coin. You understand."

She nodded. "I understand, but I don't understand why."

"Why what?"

"Why are you coming back in time? Is it just to play baseball?"

He sighed. "This was just one of the reasons. I don't get a chance to play it in my time," he said. "I found out that the boys had a field to play in the springtime which I thought would be very cool."

"Why did you come to see me?" she said, almost angrily. "You could have gone anywhere in this amazing ship. Why come here to see me? Why now at this time?"

"I told you I was researching the school history to write a book and came across the picture of your graduating class. I needed to know more. I have been working on the time ship for a long time."

She paused again, searching for the words. "You wanted to learn about me?"

"Yes."

"What did you want to know?"

"Who you are, what kind of person you are. There was no information."

"So you came across time? I'm just a regular girl. I'm not anyone important."

"I'm a doctor and an historian," Andrew smiled. "You wrote books on the school and that was what got my attention. I was writing an updated book. So you are important. Also, I wanted to test the time ship."

She paused, as if considering his words. "I write books?" she said.

"Yes, you will."

"You said if all went well, you would return," she said. "That was so many weeks ago. I thought you were not coming back."

Andrew smiled. "Yes, sorry about that, but you remembered," he said. "Yes, I was a little shook up after the trip but I recovered. The ship performed well. All systems activated. I saw that the boys played baseball at this time of year and I just had to come to play. I couldn't resist the chance to play. I wondered if I could perform in the past as I did in the present.

"You are very good."

"Thank you," he smiled.

"So what do you think of me?"

He sighed and walked up next to her. "I'm a 21th century man talking with a 19th century woman. I think that's pretty incredible. This is something that has never happened before.

Some people would think of me as a trailblazer. I don't know what I'm going to do about this yet." He paused. "There was something I wanted to ask you."

"What is that?"

"Do you want to see where I came from? My world? The future?"

She stared at him, looking dumbfounded. "I can come with you? To the 21th century? But you had said no."

"I said that to the others, but not to you. I am willing to show you the academy in the present, my present." He paused a moment, knowing it was a lot to take in. "I can have you back in ten minutes, that is ten minutes your time."

She seemed to think about it for a moment and then nodded. "Very well," she said.

"You better tell your friends. We wouldn't want them thinking I'm kidnapping you."

"I will," she said, walking down the steps and going out the door.

17

Rowena walked out the door of the ship and saw her friends standing in front of it talking with each other. She ran over to Sarah who was breathing a sigh of relief as she looked at her.

"Rowena," she said, "we were getting worried about you in there."

Rowena smiled. "I'm fine, Sarah. I've decided to go with him to the future. He said he'll have me back in ten minutes."

Sarah's eyes grew wide. "Are you sure you want to do that?" she said. "You don't know what will happen. Can you trust him?"

Rowena thought about it for a moment. Everything he had said had been true so far, why wouldn't she trust him? She began to get excited. What would she actually see there?

"Doctor Andrew Thompson, I do trust him," she smiled, "I'll see you when I get back. I'll tell you all about it." She turned and went back to the ship.

She stepped back inside the ship and Doctor Andrew was pushing some buttons on the control panel.

"So are you ready?" he said.

Rowena smiled. "Ready."

He glanced at her. "We have each other, Ro. I trust you, and you can trust me."

Rowena looked at Doctor Andrew and nodded. For the first time she saw that for a Negro, he was very handsome and very sure of himself. She had never met anyone like him before.

"I do trust you." She looked up with a weird grimace that became a laugh. "Let's go."

"Okay, here we go," he smiled. "Jennie, activate time warp systems."

"Systems activated," said a female voice.

Rowena jumped when she heard the voice. She didn't know where it came from. "What was that?"

"I'm sorry, I forget, that's the computer," said Doctor Andrew. "I named her Jennie. You'll learn about computers. Jennie, say hello to Rowena."

"Hello Rowena, welcome to the time ship."

Rowena gulped and shivered. "Hello Jennie," she said. "Thank you."

The doctor smiled and started pushing buttons and she could hear machinery humming. Something was happening. Lights began blinking on the control panel. He pulled down a lever. There was a little bump and she knew they were moving.

"Don't tell anyone you're from the past," he said, "No one knows about the time ship."

Rowena nodded, knowing that it would seem very strange to say that. She didn't want to attract any unwanted attention. Then again, that might already happen because of her. It sure happened when Doctor Andrew suddenly appeared in the girls' dorm.

The lights stopped blinking and the machinery sound stopped. Had they arrived already? Doctor Andrew shut everything down.

"Put on these glasses," he said, "These will protect your eyes just in case the sun is too much for you."

Rowena took the glasses. The lenses were dark and the frames felt like plastic. "These are for my eyes?"

"Yes."

She put the glasses on and noticed everything was a bit darker. The glasses would protect her eyes from the harshness of the environment. Maybe the light from the future time was different from hers. She could see that Doctor Andrew was taking no chances.

"Also take this," he said, handing her a metallic bracelet.

"What is this?" she said.

"It's a bracelet that's also a communicator. This is in case we get separated." He took the bracelet from her and wrapped it around her right wrist. "I will have one too. If we get separated, you press this white button and talk into it."

"Really?"

"Yes, that way we can talk to each other. It also works as a teleportation device."

She shook her head. "What is that?"

"We can contact the ship in case of emergency and Jennie can teleport us inside. That is what happened when I left the dorm weeks ago. I reappeared right in the ship."

"That is incredible. The boys said there was a bright light and you disappeared."

Doctor Andrew smiled. "That's right," he said, walking back to the control panel. "We're here. Ro, open the door and see where we are."

She liked the way he called her, Ro. It was like an endearment. Her father called her that at times. She went to the door and opened it. She stepped out into a room of desks and other scientific items, like microscopes. What was this place? The ship had moved!

When she stepped out, she realized that the ship had changed from a tree to a metal cylinder. The air smelt different; she couldn't explain it. She was in a room, a laboratory. This was truly amazing. She had changed location. She was inside a futuristic laboratory. She was really in the future. Doctor Andrew had spoken the truth.

Doctor Andrew stepped out the ship and locked the door. She noticed that he also wore a bracelet. He took a deep breath and smiled, "Doesn't the future smell delicious," he said.

"The air does smell different," she said, smiling and shaking her head. "But it is amazing. I would never have guessed this would happen."

"I'm going to show you something that's familiar," he said, moving to the window. "Many things have changed but I'll show you something familiar."

They went over to the window and looked outside. Rowena saw the Victorian building that she had come to love.

"Academy Hall!" she said. "It's still there."

"It's called Founders' Hall now," said Doctor Andrew. "It's the oldest building on campus."

Rowena was happy that the building was still there. She had always loved that building. It was good to see it.

"You want to go outside for a closer look?" he said, smiling. He seemed so pleasant. She liked his smile. "Let's go."

They left the laboratory and walked out into the hall. They went through the rear entry hall and into the main corridor. It led directly to a large room, three stories high. Glass panels covered the roof, allowing light to fill the space. Rowena noticed immediately all the activity of the people rushing back and forth. She noticed the different races of people, their clothing and the language of the school setting. There were also screens with people on them talking. People were walking around with little handheld devices. There were also other machine like creatures rolling around the floor.

"Doctor Thompson!" someone called from behind them.

"So formal, Russell?" said Doctor Andrew, without turning around.

She looked as a very tall Negro man fell in step with them.

"Hey, buddy, weren't you suppose to get a report to Doctor Winston?"

"I've been busy."

The tall Negro man looked at Rowena. "So I see," he said. "Hello. And you're also playing baseball?"

Doctor Andrew looked down at the pinstripe baseball uniform. "Oh yeah," he said, "I forgot I had these on."

"Who is this?" he said.

"Russell, this is Rowena. Russell's my best friend and he works in the Education Department."

"Hi," said Rowena, and Russell smiled.

Rowena noticed that Russell was very handsome too. She noticed that he stared at her very peculiar. She suddenly realized that she was wearing her clothes from her time. They were going to look rather different. She knew she would cause attention.

"Tell Doctor Winston I'll get that report to him later, Russell. I'm giving Rowena a tour of the school. We'll be going down to the academy too. Don't wait up for us."

Russell stopped as they kept going toward the door to the outside world. Rowena could already feel the excitement welling up inside of her just thinking about what she would see.

18

The air was pretty warm and the sun felt good too. Rowena noticed there were small flying machines around. There were also more screens with people talking on them. Many students were walking about. Some even looked at her strangely because of her dress. She did feel a little out of place but she enjoyed what she was looking at.

They made their way over to Academy Hall, or as Doctor Andrew called it, "Founders' Hall." Rowena saw that it looked even better close up. Did they paint it? The building was yellow with brown trim.

"Do you see that plaque by the building?" said Doctor Andrew.

"Yes," she said, "it says that it is an historical building."

"That's what I was saying. It's a great building. I took a Psychology class in there."

Rowena looked around. "The campus looks so different. So many new buildings."

"Yes, that building over there," he said, pointing to his right, "is the library. The building down there opposite to us is the Dining Commons or the cafeteria."

"You have many different kinds of people here, including coloreds."

"That's African Americans now. It's more politically correct. You have Irish-American, German-American. It depends on where you come from in the world."

Rowena gasped. "I'm so sorry," she said, sadly. "I guess I am a little behind the times."

He smiled at her. "It's okay," he said. "It's all so new. You're doing well."

She was happy with his approval. It was a lot to take in. "Where is East Hall?"

"East Hall doesn't exist anymore. West Hall is gone too. In fact, since your time the academy became a junior college and then a college. The academy and college separated and have their own administrations. The academy building is down the street. We'll go down and take a look."

They walked over to where many strange objects were. She didn't know what they were. They looked like they had wheels though.

"I know," he said, "you're wondering what they are. They are called automobiles or cars. They came about in the early twentieth century. The horsepower is inside the hood."

"I did wonder what they were," she said.

He went over to a car and opened a door. "This one is mine," he said, "Climb in."

Rowena looked at it for a moment and then sat down carefully inside. Doctor Andrew shut the door and walked around to the other side. He opened the door and got in next to her behind the wheel. He pulled out his own sunglasses and put them on. They looked good on him.

"The academy is down the street," he said. "I'm going to take you down there."

19

Doctor Andrew put the key in a slot and turned. The car made a strange noise and Rowena almost jumped out of her seat. She covered her ears. What a noise! "Sorry," he said. "That's the horsepower of the engine. See that belt to your right? Grab that and pull it across your body and snap it in. It's like this."

He took his belt and pulled it across his body and snapped it in. She did the same. Then they went off and her eyes popped out looking at everything. She had so many questions. The future looked fantastic.

They went down the street to the academy building. In fact, there were two buildings next to each other; the elementary school on the left and the academy on the right. There was a lot of activity there too as many cars were sitting in front of the elementary school building.

"Parents come by to pick up their children after classes," he said. "I wanted to come at this time so you could see it for yourself."

"They do this all the time?"

"Every day."

"So many people and they all have their own cars."

"Yes, that's right," he said. "Some of them fly in."

Rowena chuckled. "They fly?" she said. "You mean like a bird?"

"Yes. Russell has one of them. I haven't had mine converted yet."

"It all looks so confusing."

Doctor Andrew laughed. "It can be."

They pulled into a parking area next to the academy. It was a long brick building with a small clock tower in front of it. Doctor Andrew got out, walked around the car and opened the door, took her hand gently and helped her out. They walked up together to the front door. She saw that the students noticed she was dressed in very different clothes.

"I can see that clothing has changed a lot."

"It has to some degree," Doctor Andrew said, opening the door. "Different clothes for different things."

She shook her head, trying to process it all. "What year is this?" she said..

"Yes, it was an old coin. This is 2032. It's the 150th anniversary of the school."

Maybe his values were outdated, but he had come from an old school of thought. She was glad that men still treated women like something other than just shorter, weaker men with breasts. She was glad that men still treated a woman like a lady, opening doors for her, paying for meals, giving flowers – all those sorts of things.

As they reached the door, it burst open and a little girl about five or six years old ran out right into them. Rowena looked at her and saw the face of the tiny pretty black girl. She squatted in front of her as her dress allowed so she could be on her level.

"Hi," she said, very politely.

The little girl smiled. "Hi, I'm sorry."

"It is okay," said Rowena, smiling. "What's your name?"

"I'm Sheena."

"That's a beautiful name, Sheena. I am Rowena."

"That's a pretty dress," said Sheena.

Rowena smiled. "Thank you, Sheena. You are so nice."

The girl's mother came out the door to gather little Sheena. Rowena stood and smiled at the pretty black woman.

"I am so sorry," said the girl's mother.

"It was no trouble," said Rowena. "She's very pretty. Goodbye, Sheena."

"Goodbye, Rowena," said the little girl waving as they moved away.

As Rowena watched them go, she said to Doctor Andrew. "What a lovely girl," she said. "I have never seen anyone like her. I never had the opportunity. Thank you."

"You're welcome," said Doctor Andrew, opening the door. "It looked like you've made a friend."

They removed their sunglasses as they went up the stairs and Doctor Andrew showed her the classrooms. Rowena was amazed by the computers and the video screens. The gymnasium and weight room was incredible. There were also graduation pictures from past years.

"I didn't see one from 1888," she said.

"You would think they would have the first one but I don't see it either."

"You said you saw it in a book?"

"Yes, it must have been in someone's private collection."

As they made their way to the front door, a man called out to Doctor Andrew. He was a tall gray-haired man with a mustache.

"Doctor Thompson," he said. "It is good to see you again."

"Thank you, Mr. Johnson," Doctor Andrew said, shaking his hand. "I would like for you to meet Rowena. Rowena, this is Principal Michael Johnson."

"Good to meet you, Rowena," he said, shaking her hand. "I really like your authentic white dress. Something to do with the anniversary?"

"Yes it is," said Doctor Andrew. "It sure is."

"Have a great day," Johnson said, going back up the stairs.

Rowena watched him go and felt really good about the exchange. The people in the future were very friendly.

"I better get you back to school in your time. You have some studying to do."

20

They returned back to the year 1888. Andrew studied the controls as the ship came to rest. He had wanted to bring Rowena back in ten minutes after they left even though they had spent more time in the future. He looked at the controls and saw that he had done just that.

"You're back," he said, "and right on time. What did you think?"

"Very impressive," she said, handing him the glasses and the bracelet. "Thank you very much. I don't know what to say."

Andrew looked at her. She did look rather pretty. He was just happy that he was able to get her back to her time in good shape. "Ro, can I come to your graduation?"

She smiled at him. "Of course, that would be nice."

"I'm glad you were able to see my home and my time. I don't know if I'll get in any trouble for it but I'm glad you were there."

She frowned. "What trouble?"

He frowned. "The whole thing with the stream of time," he said. "I'm not supposed to be here and yet I am. You're not supposed to be in the future and yet you were."

She thought about that. "I see what you mean."

"We'll see what happens," he said, clicking buttons. "Let's go see your friends. They're waiting for you."

They went out the door and her friends were still standing there. Sarah ran over to them. "Rowena," she said, "the tree disappeared right before our eyes. I don't know what to say. And then ten minutes later, it reappeared." Sarah shook her head. "You're simply glowing. Are you all right?"

"Yes, Sarah," smiled Rowena. "Doctor Andrew took me to the future. It was wonderful."

Andrew felt a little out of place there but he enjoyed the enthusiasm her schoolmates showed as they crowded around her to hear about the future. He studied her carefully. He saw that she was excited. There seemed to be no ill effects from the trip on her. She had traveled to the future and back to her own time unharmed. He hoped she would stay that way. He didn't want her to have brought a plague from the future into the past. That would have been catastrophic.

"Ro, I've got to go," he said, moving back to the ship. "I'll see you for your graduation. Study hard and make me proud."

Rowena followed him to the door. Andrew turned and faced her. She was smiling. "Do you have to go?"

"Yes, I better get back and do my reports and get ready for my classes. I teach Physics."

"I will miss you," she said, softly. "Thank you so much."

"Thank you, Rowena Michaels, for a chance to be with you. I look forward to seeing you soon again. I need to interview you for my book." He looked at the ship. "I have to go inside my tree and make it disappear again before your teachers show up."

"True."

"Bye, Ro."

"Bye, Doctor Andrew."

He smiled and gave her a little kiss on the cheek and dashed inside. He closed the door and took a deep breath. Wow, this was getting interesting. It seemed that every time he came back in time he stirred the pot a little more. He didn't know where this was heading but he had to be careful. He went up to the control panel and punched in the information for home.

"Jennie," he said.

"Yes, doctor.".

"It's time to go home," he said. "Punch it."

He had one more thought of Rowena and pulled the lever. The ship hummed and began its trip.

21

Rowena's mind was in a fog. What had happened? She was perfectly happy with her life just going along and doing her studies and preparing to be a teacher. Then Doctor Andrew showed up and showed her the future. Now her whole world was turned upside down.

When she slept at night, her dreams were filled with images of what she had seen in his time. She saw the buildings, people, cars, clothing, and a whole new world. She imagined what it would be like to live in that time. It had to be very different. Just from what she had seen in the few minutes she was there, it was not only exciting but she felt so out of place. Then she would return to her time and everything seemed so dark and backwards. The future looked so bright and new.

She tried to talk to Sadie and Sarah and even Carla about it but they would frown and not want to listen. All they wanted to do was talk about Doctor Andrew.

"How could you go away with that Negro?" said Sadie. "He could have hurt you. You shouldn't have gone by yourself."

"It just isn't natural, I tell you," said Sarah. "He even touched you, kissed you."

"Where does he come from?" said Carla.

"Who would go to see a Negro doctor anyway?" said Sadie.

"He's not a regular doctor," said Rowena. "He's a scientist interested in space."

"You mean like outer space?" said Carla. "Isn't that science fiction?"

"It is very real. I saw so much," said Rowena. "I saw little machines flying around. Students were there from all over the world. I saw the school buildings. The school is going to grow bigger. People were very nice."

She felt so alone. Her world seems so backwards now. Even the younger students were talking about her. Was Doctor Andrew really from the future or was he just crazy? She knew what she saw. She had experienced it. She even remembered the little black girl she had run into. Sheena. She was real.

She sat down and wrote to her parents. They needed to know what had happened. Would they think she was crazy? Her parents were practical people but they never had her around Negroes at all. Why would she make this up? It had to be real. Others saw him and they went into the time ship. She was so confused. She just didn't understand what it meant to her. The photograph was the catalyst. When he handed her the picture and the coin, her whole world changed.

Her teachers were staring at her too. They did not come out and say anything bad but she knew what they were thinking. They thought she was crazy and it was all a matter of time before one of them said something to Principal Bell and she would be in trouble.

She had no answer to this.

Rowena went to see Miss Daniels, her literature teacher. Miss Daniels was her advisor and mentor while she was in school. The teacher had blonde hair piled high and was dressed in a pink long sleeved dress with the high collar. Rowena thought maybe Miss Daniels would have some idea about this.

"I don't know what to think, Rowena," she said. "He just came out of nowhere?"

"He did," said Rowena, as they sat in the teacher's office. "I do know that I went into the future and I saw many incredible things. A few of us even went into the time ship. It's real. He's real."

Miss Daniels looked at her for a moment. "I guess we won't know until he returns. He has certainly stirred things up here. If he is who he says he is, this could change everything we know about the world and the universe."

"What can I do?"

"That's the question. The only thing you can do is learn as much as you can. If he does come back, he's coming to see you. He's writing a book about the school? You need to find out more about him. He apparently wants to know more about you."

"It is so strange."

"Yes, I know. Don't be afraid, Rowena. You have already traveled with him. Do you trust him?"

Rowena thought a moment. He had asked the same question. Even Sarah had asked that. She had traveled alone with him and he had been kind to her. She even wondered if he had fallen in love with her. "I do trust him," she said. "He's a good man and has treated me well."

Miss Daniels nodded. "Then when he does come back, he will come to you and you can learn more about him. He has some kind of power. We don't understand it. But if he can travel through time you will know about what it means very soon."

Rowena sighed. "Is it possible that he likes me?"

Miss Daniels paused again, probably trying to find the words to say. How can a Negro like a respectful white girl? "It's possible," she said. "Maybe things are different in the future. From what you said, the world definitely looks different. The answers will come, Rowena. They will come."

22

Sarah Bell knew something was wrong with Rowena. They had been friends all their lives and she never acted like this. What was wrong with her? Why was she hanging around with this Negro man? It just was not natural. What could be done about this?

She didn't know what else to do so she went to see Principal Richard Bell. Even though they had the same last name they were not related. Bell had an office in Academy Hall as did the other teachers. She had to steak her case to the principal. Mrs. Knowles had said some weeks before that she was going to talk to the principal about this.

They met in his office. Principal Bell was a tall man with a full dark beard. He was well liked by everyone. He sat behind the desk and faced Sarah.

"What is it that you need, Miss Bell?"

"It's about the colored man who has come to see Rowena Michaels."

Bell nodded. "Yes," he said. "I've heard about him from several people, including Mr. Walker and Mrs. Knowles. It seems as though he has come back again."

"Yes sir. Something needs to be done about him."

"Has he done something to Miss Michaels that we need to address?"

"Well, he did touch her hand when he first came. And now recently, he kissed her cheek. Things like this should not be allowed."

"Indeed, Miss Bell. Very true. But what can we do? He comes in and then he disappears."

Sarah thought about what she had seen inside the time ship and then seeing it disappear. There was so much she didn't understand. Yet, she pushed all of that aside and focused on her present situation. This was not right. "He should be arrested," she said.

"Arrested?"

"Yes sir. He should not be allowed to be around her."

"What of Miss Michaels? What does she say?"

Sarah paused again, but pressed on. "She goes on about him being from the future and how he took her there. This is not natural, Doctor Bell. He's supposed to be a doctor and he appears and disappears. Rowena even invited him to the graduation."

Doctor Bell stroked his beard. "This is a situation all right," he said.

"You should call the sheriff and have him arrested at the graduation."

"Do you really think we should do all of that? Is that necessary?"

"Yes, Doctor Bell, this is very important," said Sarah. "We need to stop him."

"Very well, Miss Bell, I will look into it. It is true we cannot have this sort of thing on campus."

"Thank you, sir. I do appreciate this."

"Good day, Miss Bell."

"Good day, sir."

Sarah left the office and walked out the building. She kept thinking that she had done something wrong but then she pushed those thoughts away thinking this was for the greater good. Rowena would thank her. Negroes needed to know their place and she didn't want her friend getting hurt from this.

23

Rowena nervously stepped toward Academy Hall. She remembered how it looked in the future and smiled thinking of how well the building would be preserved. It was more of a gray color now compared to the yellow color in the future. She had been summoned by Principal Bell on an urgent matter. She had no idea what it could have been about. Was she in trouble for something?

She walked into his office and he stood from behind his desk. Bell smiled through his manicured black beard and gray eyes. He had the features of a man accustomed to having his way. Everyone loved him. Rowena liked the principal also. So by being there it had to be serious.

"Please have a seat, Miss Michaels," he said.

Rowena sat and stared up solemnly at the principal. She remembered Principal Michael Johnson in the future. He was very nice too.

"I understand," he said, "that you have been seen in the company of a mysterious colored man."

Rowena took a deep breath. She was afraid it would came to this someday. "I may have crossed paths with him," she said.

"You did more than cross paths, my dear. He came to see you with a message and now he frequents the campus."

She shook her head. "He has been here a couple of times."

"We're hoping to get a few Negro students here in the future. We have talks with officials in Bermuda and in Jamaica. Maybe even in New York and Boston."

"That would be good," she said, cautiously.

Bell sat down at his desk and looked at her. Rowena could feel the hairs on the back of her neck stand up. Was this the trouble that Doctor Andrew spoke about? "He has caused a fervor around the campus. Everyone is talking about him," he said. "It has been said that he appears and disappears. Where does he come from? Does he live here in the community?"

"I don't know."

"Rowena, I will have him arrested when he returns here."

"Why?" she cried. "He's not hurting anyone."

"Maybe," said the principal, softly, "but we cannot have strange men speaking with our academy ladies."

"Is this because he is a Negro?"

Bell shook his head. "This has nothing to do with his ethnicity," he said. "But we must be protected."

"I don't understand this, Doctor Bell, Doctor Andrew has done nothing."

"That's another thing," he said. "What's he's a doctor of?"

"Physics."

"So he says."

"Doctor Bell, what do you want me to say? He's been here a couple of times and he's played baseball with the boys. He has not done anything wrong."

"That's all, Miss Michaels."

Rowena realized the meeting was over. She stood, smoothed out her dress, and left the office. When she left Academy Hall, she met Sarah walking by outside. She still could not get the meeting out of her mind. Why would Principal Bell have the sheriff arrest Doctor Andrew? How could she possibly warn him?

"Hi, Rowena," called Sarah. "What happened to you?"

"I can't believe Principal Bell wants Doctor Andrew arrested."

Sarah grunted. "I told you it's not natural," she said. "You know that."

Rowena stared at her friend. She had an uneasy feeling about this. "Did you have anything to do with this, Sarah?"

Sarah frowned. "I was the one who contacted the principal and he is going to call the sheriff."

Rowena shook her head. "But why?"

"I don't want you to get hurt. He's not good for you."

"Sarah, you went inside the time ship. You know he's a good man. You saw the ship disappear and reappear. You know all about it. How could you?" Rowena said, and then she walked away.

24

Walker made his way to Andrew Thompson's lab late in the evening. He had been watching him carefully and waited for him to leave for home. There was a lot of activity in the lab. Something was happening in there and he would find out what it was.

Walker noticed over the past several days that Thompson would stay very late into the night. Winston had given him a key so he went up to the door and turned the lock. The door opened with no problem and he stepped inside.

The room was dark and he dared not risk turning on the light so he clicked on his flashlight and took a look around. Winston had told him to find out what was in there that dealt with time.

He searched the room carefully and walked around the desks. He did not see anything out of the ordinary. It was just a regular lab with the equipment scattered around on the tables. He then came to a metal object that looked like a cylinder. He placed his hand on it and thought he felt something pulsing. There was something inside. Maybe this was what Winston was talking about.

He walked around and saw the keyhole for the cylinder. There was no way he would be able to get in. He pushed the door but it was locked. He needed that key.

"Intruder alert!" said a female voice.

Walker almost leaped out of his shoes. His blood pressure almost went through the roof. His heart was pounding. Where did that come from? He had to get out of there.

"Intruder alert!" it said again. "Initiating security protocols. "

Walker ran toward the door. He ran into the table. It was time to get out. He didn't know what it was but it was important enough to have security protocols for it.

He got out of the lab, locked the door, and went to Winston's office. The man was still working, burning the midnight oil. He walked in and Winston looked up, almost startled by him and the look on his face. Walker sat in the chair in front of the desk out of breath.

"What did you find?" said Winston.

"There is something in there, a cylinder. It had a low hum. When I touched it, a female voice sounded the intruder alert. I got out of there," Walker said, thinking a deep breath to calm himself. "What if the cameras picked it up? Even in the dark I could get into big trouble."

Winston shook his head. "I don't think he had any cameras there so you shouldn't have to worry," he said. "What do you think?"

"If it is a time machine, we need more evidence. The cylinder door was locked."

"Understood," said Winston, calmly. "I don't think I'll be able to get in there again but I'll think of something."

25

Russell Kingston stepped into Doctor Robert Winston's office with a little wave of nervousness. Was he in trouble for something? What was he doing here? This wasn't even his department. He wondered if it had anything to do with Andrew. It had to be about Andrew. He sat down in the chair near Marsha, Winston's secretary, and pondered what was going to happen to him. She was a young, neatly dressed black woman, wearing a tight stylish high ponytail.

"Doctor Winston will see you now, Doctor Kingston," she said.

He took a deep breath and stood up. He walked into the large office and found the bearded man behind the desk. "Good afternoon, Doctor Kingston, have a seat."

"Thank you, sir," he said, nervously.

"I guess you're wondering why I called you in. I was not aware that Doctor Thompson had a leave of absence."

"Sir?"

"It seems that he has been doing a few other things beside his regular workload."

"I don't think I understand what you mean."

"There is speculation that Thompson is doing something in his lab that is not sanctioned by the college. He was also seen with a young woman who was dressed in 19th century clothing recently."

Russell had also seen her and noticed how much she looked like the picture of one of the girls Andrew had shown him in that book on the history of the school. He was researching the material for a book he was writing. The girl was wearing sunglasses. But how could that be? He had a lot of questions himself.

"As his friend," Winston continued, "I wanted you to let him know that I'm looking to talk to him. The administrators may want to take a look in his lab too," said Winston.

"Doctor Winston, I want you to know that I do not know what Andrew is doing inside his lab. We are in different departments. He does not share his physics projects with me."

Winston stared at him. "I know that, Kingston," he said, sternly. "Just help me out a bit."

When Russell left the office, his head was spinning. What was going on? It was like he was in the middle of a conspiracy. Was this about the secret project Andrew was working on?

He went down the hall to Andrew's lab. Was he even there? He walked into the lab and found Andrew writing something in a notebook and then imputing it into his computer.

"Andrew, buddy, Winston is mad and he's on to you."

"What do you mean?" said Andrew, clicking buttons.

"I mean, he wants to know what you're doing in here. He plans on taking a look."

Andrew pushed back from the desk and rubbed his eyes. "I guess the time has come."

"What's going on?"

"There's something I have to show you, Russell, and it's in that cylinder. You have to promise not to tell anyone."

"I definitively promise," said Russell. "I just knew that it's apparently important."

Andrew stood and walked towards it. There was a sadness about him. Russell didn't know what to make of this. "I'm going to show you what I've been working on for the past eight years. I knew I would have to sooner or later."

Andrew opened the cylinder door with a key. The door swung open and Russell saw something that completely blew his mind. How did he get all that machinery in there? It looked so big.

"I knew you were smart, buddy, but this is amazing."

"I know," Andrew said. "It's bigger on the inside than the outside. Wanta go inside?"

"Sure."

Russell stepped into the cylinder and looked around. It was definitely bigger on the inside. He looked at the control panel and still didn't know what was going on.

"Andrew, what is this?"

"It's a time ship."

"Time ship? You mean like a time machine?"

"Yeah, I've made a couple of trips already."

"So Winston was right," said Russell. "He knows something about this, but obviously he hasn't seen it yet. That's why he's bringing the administration in on it."

"I realize if he does, I could be out of business," said Andrew, sullenly. "There's something I have to show you."

Andrew took Russell through a door and down a hallway. He still couldn't believe how big the place was. He had walked into a cylinder and now he was in a different location. How could this be?

"Where are we going?" he said.

Andrew came to a door. "Let me show you."

He opened the door into a large room where Russell saw a bright ball with metal bands swinging round it. He put his arms up to shield his eyes because of the brightness.

"What is it?" he cried.

"It's a sphere," said Andrew. "This is what opened up the dimensional vortex for me. This is why we can walk in here like this."

"Incredible."

"Yeah, it developed over a few years," said Andrew. "I had to harness it in a way that I could use it. My roommate Sean had said we had to open a door into a new dimension. He had this vision before he died. This definitely changed my life."

Russell could feel his mind, thinking. He was so overwhelmed by this. "Wait a minute, that girl you were walking with the other day," he said. "She was dressed in that ancient dress. I knew she looked familiar. That picture from the book you showed me. You're going to the past in this thing?"

Andrew nodded. "Yes, I have. As I said, I've made a couple of trips. It's amazing, Russell, I've gone back to the year 1888."

Russell just didn't understand that. "Why would you go into the past?" he said. "Isn't it dangerous? What if you went back in time and got killed? What if you were enslaved and couldn't get back?"

Andrew smiled. "Don't worry, buddy," he said. "I've thought of all of that. I know there are risks but it's going to be all right."+

"And you've brought back someone from the past?" Russell shook his head. "If this gets out to Winston there will be a lot of trouble. He's seen the girl, he's suspicious."

"That's why I'm going to need you to cover for me. Winston's going to want to come in here to take a look inside here. I'll need you to do something special for me."

Russell smiled. "Partners in crime, I like that."

26

Rowena studied hard. She didn't want to miss a step. She wanted to graduate with honors and now not only would her parents be there but also the man from beyond tomorrow. She wrote her parents about him and who he was. She didn't think they would believe her. Now that he was coming to her graduation they would be able to meet him. She wondered what their reactions would be to him. It was an incredible story, but she had learned so much about him and the time he lived in. She hoped he didn't get into any trouble. She worried though that he would be arrested when he came.

She was walking with Sarah back to the dorm. She was always thinking about the campus she saw in the future compared to this one. There were so many changes that would happen over the years and the school would eventually become a college.

"What are you thinking about, Rowena?"

"Nothing, really." Rowena said, snapping back to the present.

"You seem far away. You're thinking about that colored man from the future again."

"No, I'm not."

Sarah smiled. "I'm beginning to know that look."

Rowena realized she couldn't hide the look. She liked the fact that she had seen the future. It was a part of her now. "If you would have seen what I had seen, Sarah, you would have been amazed," she said.

"Well, I still think it's unnatural."

"Why don't you like him?" Rowena said. "Why do you want him arrested?"

"I'm sorry, Rowena, but why should I like him? He comes out of nowhere and starts talking to you. He's touched you. He doesn't act the way he should. It's not natural. People like him do not talk like that to people like you."

"Sarah, he's from another time," said Rowena. "You know that."

They walked into the dorm and were about to go up the stairs to their rooms when the freckle-faced blonde girl at the desk called out to them.

"Stop!" the girl called.

Rowena and Sarah stopped and looked back at her. "What is it, Daniela?" said Rowena.

Daniela went behind the desk and pulled out a bouquet of a dozen yellow roses in a red vase. "These are for you, Rowena," she said. "The colored man who first came to see you stopped by to drop them off."

Rowena almost went into shock. "Doctor Andrew was here?" she smiled.

"He sent you flowers?" said Sarah, shaking her head.

They walked over to the desk and Rowena took a look at them. "They are beautiful," she said, examining them. "These are not from around here. These are from the future."

"How are they from the future?" said Daniela, shaking her head.

Sarah looked at Daniela, sullenly. "Don't get her started about that."

Rowena smelt the flowers and smiled. She was very happy. No one had ever sent her an arrangement of flowers before. She looked at the address and the date on the roses. It was sent from a place just down the road but the date was April 22, 2032.

27

Rowena thought it was unbelievable that Doctor Andrew had sent her flowers from the future. She was still thinking about that kiss he gave her. She had never been kissed before either. Then Doctor Andrew sent the flowers. Was he in love with her from across time?

The flowers were very nice. The roses lasted many, many days and they smelt great too. Many of the other girls stopped by her room when they heard and told her the flowers looked great. They were amazed as she was about the fact that they were from the future. The fact that he had brought them to her from the future made her smile. She wished she could thank him. But he wouldn't be born for more than a hundred years. It sounded strange just thinking that. What in the world could she do? She had to think of something.

Then she thought of something while she was walking with Sarah and Robin to the dorm. This was something totally unheard of. It was almost impossible to think it were possible to do. What if she could send him a note in the future?

"I can send Doctor Andrew a letter," she said.

Sarah laughed. "You can't do that," she said. "He's not even born yet even though he comes to see you."

"I'm going to try. Maybe something can be held over at the post office. You know, it can be delivered to him in the future."

"Wait a minute," said Robin, a dark-haired junior, "you have a boyfriend from the future?"

"And a colored one too," said Sarah.

"He is not my boyfriend," said Rowena. "And I think the phrase is African American."

"Whatever it is," said Sarah, "you can't send him a letter."

Rowena thought for a moment. "I may have an idea."

Rowena went to the post office and spoke with Samuel Whitfield, the Postmaster General. He was a small elderly man who was well respected in the community. If anyone could help her, she thought, he could.

"Mr. Whitfield," she said, as they sat in his office. "I want to send a letter."

"That's no problem, Rowena. You don't need me for that."

"I do for this type of letter, sir. I want to know if the postal service can hold a letter for delivery at a later date."

"Yes, I have heard of that happening. It's called postdating," Whitfield said, preparing to write. "What is the date of the letter?"

"Well, it's going to be in the year 2032."

Whitfield almost dropped his pen. "What did you say?" he said, staring at her.

Rowena took a breath. "I know it sounds crazy, but I need the letter delivered in 2032."

He eyed her carefully. "Is this some kind of joke?"

"No, Mr. Whitfield, I assure you this is not a joke. I need a letter delivered to a certain address in the year 2032. I will get you the exact date. It will be delivered to a person who will be working at this school at that time."

"In the year 2032?"

"Yes, sir."

Whitfield sighed. "I thought I had heard everything."

"It will be okay, Mr. Whitfield. I will help you with the information."

Rowena knew that it sounded weird. She didn't even know if it would even work. Yet she wanted so much to get the letter to him. It was so sweet and he would be coming to her graduation. She also had to warn him about the sheriff. He would have to watch himself that he wouldn't be arrested.

28

Andrew was working in his lab after class when a man came in looking to see him. The man was dressed as a courtier and he had a small bag in his hand. Andrew looked at him, curiously.

"Doctor Andrew Thompson?" he said.

"Yes?" said Andrew, straightening up to look at him.

"Are you Doctor Andrew Thompson?" he repeated.

"Yes I am."

The man frowned. "I am from Western Union Telegrams," he said. "I have been commissioned to come see you because we have in our possession a letter addressed to you to be delivered at this particular place on this particular date."

Andrew shook his head. This was strange. "A real letter? No one does letters anymore."

"Very true," he said, opening the bag and pulling out an old envelope. "Yet this one has been in our possession for 144 years. We didn't know if we would actually meet you. We took bets in the office. I guess I lost." He smiled.

The man handed him the letter and Andrew signed for it before the man showed himself out. Andrew carefully opened the letter, careful not to destroy any of the contents. This was so strange. This was such an old letter. What did it mean? He hoped he was not in any trouble.

When he began to read the letter he realized it was from Rowena. But how did she do this? How did she get a letter to Western Union to be held for so long? How did she know when and where to send it?

He began to read the full letter.

"Dear Doctor Andrew,

"I wanted to write you this letter to thank you for the beautiful flowers you gave to me. They were very lovely and completely unexpected. To think they had come from the future. I displayed them in my room and received many complements from the other girls. They were amazed when I told them the flowers came from you and were from the future. They really do want to meet you.

"You are a sweet caring man and I am so blessed to have met you. Please come back for the graduation. I am studying hard and it looks as though I will graduate with honors. I cannot wait to see you. This is so strange to write to you years before you are even born. Even Sarah thinks it is crazy.

By the way, be careful because Principal Bell said that he has instructed the sheriff to arrest you when you come back. He didn't like the idea of you being around the campus and around me. Let me tell you that I do not mind your presence a bit.

"Take care, my love, and I will see you soon."
Love, Ro.

Andrew almost cried as he read the letter. She had thought of writing him a letter and making sure he would get it at a particular time and place. How did she understand to do that? He shook his head. He had delivered the flowers and she had read the card. The date was on it. She was an incredible woman. She had called him "my love." Did she love him? Was that possible? He couldn't wait to see her again. This was very impressive. He couldn't miss her graduation. He didn't have a suit from the period. He would have to make do with what he had. Then he thought. Maybe since the anniversary celebration was going on there would be a 19th century suit he could borrow for the trip. He would check with the anniversary committee about that. Then he could blend in, well, at least as far as the clothes. He was still him. The sheriff and the impending arrest made him nervous. Who turned him in? He thought everyone liked him.

29

Rowena was in her room preparing for graduation. The next day would be her graduation and she was preparing for the beginning of her future life. While she was cleaning up the room, and putting things in order, Sarah came by the door. Rowena looked up and saw the sadness written across her friend's face. Her heart went out to her. What had happened? She knew that the two of them had not seen eye to eye about Doctor Andrew. But she was still her best friend and she was concerned about her. Rowena laid aside her broom.

"What's wrong, Sarah?"

"Rowena, I've been all wrong about you," she said, tears flowing down her cheeks.

Rowena shook her head. She had not expected the tears. "What are you talking about? Wrong about what?"

Sarah walked in and sat on the bed. She wiped her tears away. "You've had an experience that I wish I could have had and I've been very mean to you."

"Tell me, Sarah, what are you talking about?" Rowena said, sitting next to her.

Tears in her eyes, Sarah said, "I've talked bad about your doctor friend from the future because he was colored and I'm sorry."

"Sarah, it's okay."

"No, it's not!" she cried. "You're right, he is a good man, your Andrew. He's ten times better than any of these boys here. I mean, it seems a little creepy about the time stuff. I tried to forget about the ship but I couldn't. It was impressive. It really was. I'm sorry about the sheriff and the principal."

"Tomorrow's our graduation, Sarah, and Doctor Andrew's coming. You're going to have him arrested during the ceremony?"

"I'll talk to Principal Bell. I'm sorry, please forgive me."

"Already done," Rowena said, hugging her friend.

"I wish I could meet someone like him. Would he have any friends?"

Rowena looked Sarah in the eye and smiled. "He may have one," she said.

"Really?"

"Yes, I met him when I was in the future. Very tall man. He seemed very nice. Maybe I'll talk with Doctor Andrew about it."

Sarah smiled and wiped her tears. "Could you, Rowena?"

"Sure," Rowena smiled. "Now, don't forget to talk to Principal Bell and the sheriff."

Sarah nodded. "I won't forget," she said. "Did you really send that letter?"

Rowena smiled and nodded. "Yes, I did. He's going to get it 144 years from now."

Sarah shook her head. "As I said, it's a bit creepy."

Rowena saw the truth in that and hugged her friend again. "All will be well, Sarah, all will be well."

30

Andrew arrived at the coordinates on graduation day for Rowena. He had spoken to Hailey and Larry from the anniversary committee and they had found a suit from the 1880s for him to borrow for the trip. He was forever grateful to them. He never told them about the time machine or why he really needed the suit because that would have really stirred up everything. He couldn't publish his findings because he would be laughed right out of the academic community. He thought about all that had happened. But then she found a way to send a message that took over one hundred and forty years to get to him. Very impressive.

He also remembered the warning she had about the sheriff. Would they be waiting for him with handcuffs when he appeared? When he landed he peeked out the door to see if anyone was around. He noticed that no one was around and he was safe to leave. So he stepped out and locked the door. It would have been interesting if someone would have seen him walking out and then locking a tree. One thing he didn't want was to end up in a nineteenth century jail for trespassing or insanity.

Andrew found the auditorium, went inside, and stood in the back. It was a small place but people were coming in. He realized that it was not going to be possible for him to keep a low profile. He was the only person of color there. Well, someone had to integrate this gathering. Also, everyone seemed to know who he was anyway, both students and teachers. Some of the girls even walked up to him mentioning the flowers he had sent to Rowena and how beautiful they were. Some people even asked about the future. He could see that he had made an impression here. Someone had probably already told Rowena that he was there.

While Andrew was standing there, a man, probably in his fifties, wearing an old style police uniform and a badge, stood behind him. The hair on the back of his neck stood up. Was it going to happen now?

"Hi there," he said. "I'm the sheriff. We were supposed to arrest you when we saw you. But that has been cancelled. The person had a change of heart. Enjoy the graduation."

The sheriff moved away from him and Andrew breathed a sigh of relief. He thought he was going to have to ask Jennie to teleport him quickly to the ship. He still didn't know who had turned him in. Now the person had changed their mind? Well, looked like things were getting better.

As he stood there, another man walked up to him wearing an impressive manicured beard. He stepped up to Andrew and held out his hand. Andrew looked at him and shook his hand..

"I am Doctor Richard Bell," the man said. "I am the principal of this school."

Andrew smiled. "Doctor Bell, it is good to meet you. Rowena has talked about you."

Bell studied Andrew for a moment. "I just want to tell you that I am sorry I have misjudged you. I hear that you are a doctor of physics and an historian in the future."

"Yes sir, right here in this school. My research led me here."

"This is an honor, sir," said Bell. "If there is anything I can do to help, please let me know."

"Thank you, sir."

"You do realize that we had certain ideals towards your people."

"America is a great country, Doctor Bell. It has come a long way but we can still learn from each other."

"Very true," Bell said.

Andrew cleared his throat. "Also sir, it was not my intention to cause any trouble with Rowena or with any of the students on this campus. If I have done anything to hurt you or anyone else here, I am truly sorry and I ask for your forgiveness."

Bell smiled and nodded. "Thank you, Doctor Thompson. You are welcome here. After all, this will be your school soon here anyway."

It was a very nice program with the school song, prayer and speeches and the four girls who would make history as the first graduating class at Beacon Academy. These were the days that he was glad he had made the time machine. The four girls sang a lovely song. They were dressed in white graduation robes and stood about the same size, very petite.

They took pictures of everyone. They wanted to take a picture of him. He didn't want to do that and yet he allowed a picture to be taken.

"I guess I'll see that one again," he said.

After the service, Andrew walked over to Rowena and hugged her. "It's good to see you again," he said. "Congratulations. I am so proud of you. I got your message. Sending it postmarked by Western Union was very creative."

"I'm so happy you got the message," she said. "I didn't know what else to do." She looked to her left at an older couple. "Doctor Andrew, these are my parents, Mr. and Mrs. James Michaels."

He was slightly nervous meeting her parents. He knew it would have happened sooner or later. He bowed slightly. "Glad to meet you."

"You're the one Rowena's been writing about," said her father. He had a magnificent dark beard.

"I am."

"You're the time traveler," said her father. "Why should we trust you?"

Andrew didn't know how to respond to that. He didn't know what the man's intentions were. "I don't know," he said. "I'm really harmless. At least that's what I've been told."

Rowena laughed. Her father looked at him, curiously. "Maybe you could show us your ship?" he said.

Andrew was a little surprised at the request but he definitely was not surprised. Then he thought, if your daughter is talking about traveling through time you needed to check it out. He took them over to the tree which got crazy looks from other onlookers who didn't know the backstory. He smiled as he opened the door of the time ship and they walked into the control room.

Mr. Michaels looked shocked as he rubbed his beard. "I guess everything I heard was true," he said. "It's bigger on the inside than on the outside."

"Yes sir, it is."

"You did this?" he said, incredulously.

"Yes sir, I did."

Andrew could tell he didn't seem convinced. He didn't think the man would give him any credit. He had to remember it was the period of time he had stepped into. This was the mindset of many toward black people at this time. Blacks were seen as sub-human or not even human and were often terrorized.

Mr. Michaels nodded and stroked his beard. "Maybe this nigger can take us to the future," he said. "I would like to see that."

Andrew shivered when he heard that. He never thought he would ever be faced with this type of racism. He had read about it but never faced it. While it was true that people hated because of color, gender, religious or national origin, he had never thought much about it. James Michaels was a racist who had grown up thinking this way and couldn't help it. He looked at Rowena who looked very embarrassed. Her mother didn't really like it either. Andrew shook his head and set the coordinates for his time.

"Jennie, coordinates set for present time and location," he said. "Take us home."

"Confirmed," said the female A. I. voice.

Rowena's parents shivered at hearing the disembodied voice. They looked at each other, terrified.

Andrew didn't offer any explanation about Jennie. Rowena would probably tell them about it. He scowled at Mr. Michaels. "Then so be it." And he pulled down the lever.

The lights flicked on and off and the machinery was activated. They were leaving the past moving through the vortex again.

31

Rowena could not believe what her father had said as they were heading to the future. She had not known her father's attitude concerning African Americans. She only knew that he was involved with the Civil War in some respects before she was born.

She was sorry that this had happened because Doctor Andrew was affected. She had grown to like him and didn't want him to be hurt. But he was obviously hurt by her father's words.

They arrived in what Doctor Andrew called "present time." They received their complementary glasses to guard their eyes from the sun and the communication bracelets. Her parents were amazed that they had reappeared inside a building and that the time ship had changed into a cylinder. Everything she went through, they were going through. Through all in all, Doctor Andrew was a true professional, showing her parents Academy Hall and then taking them down the road in the car to the academy building.

Her father was very impressed. At first, he thought it was an illusion, a trick. There was so much to see. But there was something that Rowena wanted to ask him.

"Father, you need to apologize to Doctor Andrew for what you said."

Her father looked confused. "What did I say?" he said.

"You know what you said, right, Mother?"

Her mother nodded. "Yes, dear, James, you did say it," she said.

Her father thought about it and realized they were right. "How was I to know?" he said.

"And now that you've seen?" said Rowena.

"I should apologize. Apparently in the future, many things change."

"Yes they do," said her mother.

Her father went to Doctor Andrew and apologized for his unkind words. Doctor Andrew accepted the apology even though he still looked hurt. Rowena wished there was something she could say or do but that was not even close to possible. One thing that happened while they were touring the school, because she still wore her white graduation robe, the principal, Mr. Johnson, seeing her again and with her parents, said that she looked like an angel. That was very sweet.

32

Andrew was called to Doctor Winston's office. It had been awhile since he was summoned to the great office. Doctor Robert Winston was the head of the Center for Theoretical Physics and Andrew had tried hard to avoid him. It looked like his time had come as he walked into the outer office where his secretary, Marsha, was. It was times like this he wished he had an excuse to visit Maria Salazar.

Winston had him wait there in the outer office for a few minutes before calling him in. Andrew walked into the large office with goosebumps. He didn't know what Winston was up to. Now that Russell knew about the time ship he could cover him. But maybe his time had run out.

He liked Winston. He liked being part of this department. He knew that what he was doing could be seen as unethical, but it was his project and he would not change a thing. He would do anything he could to protect it. If he told Winston about it, the chairman would shut him down and steal his project.

Doctor Winston sat behind his enormous desk and studied Andrew for a moment. "Doctor Thompson," he said, in his baritone voice, "good you could come. Please, have a seat."

Andrew sat down in the chair in front of the desk waiting for the hammer to drop. Was he being let go? Was he in any trouble? "Thank you, Doctor Winston, what can I do for you, sir?"

Winston studied him carefully for a moment. "What are you doing in that lab?" he said, sternly.

"What do you mean, sir, I'm just working."

"Yes, but there's something else."

Andrew wondered if he suspected anything. Doctor Winston was a smart man and he always seemed to be in control. Russell was right. He would find out about the time ship sooner or later and when he did, he would have his head. Winston could do anything, even have surveillance robots or drones flying around.

"Something else, sir?"

"Yes," Winston said, standing. He started to pace a little behind his desk. "I've noticed that you have spent a lot of time in your lab. Working on anything important?"

"No, just the usual."

"I've also noticed that you have had guests dressed in 19th century clothing. Very interesting."

Andrew blinked. Russell was right. Winston was watching him. "Yes sir, they were part of the anniversary celebration."

Winston stopped pacing and looked at him. Andrew felt the man's eyes penetrating his very soul. He shivered. The hammer was about to drop. "Are you sure there isn't anything you would like to tell me? Anything?"

Andrew paused as if thinking. Was Winston giving him a chance to turn himself in? "No, not really," he said. "Everything is good. I'm getting ready for my physics class and you'll be happy to hear that everyone is doing well."

Winston frowned, probably expecting something else. "Yes, I'm sure," he said.

"Can I go now?" he said, aware as soon as he said it that he was sounding like a small child.

Winston scowled. "Yes, you can."

Andrew stood and left the room. What was going on? Was he being watched?

When Andrew was gone, Winston sat staring at the framed photos of Roxanne and the kids. It seemed inevitable that he had to do something drastic. Thompson was hiding something that would change everything. He just needed the proof. Even with the best of intentions come risks. He just had to take some.

33

When Andrew walked into the lobby of the nursing home, the man at the desk almost went cross-eyed looking at him. It was now 1959 and Andrew walked up to the startled attendant who probably thought he was lost. Why would there be a black man walking into the building? Andrew thought the attendant would also be wondering about the strange purple and white uniform he was wearing.

"I would like to see Miss Rowena Michaels, please."

The man, who looked to be around forty with short dark hair, frowned at him. "Does she know you?" he growled.

"I'm an old friend of the family," Andrew sneered. He realized that prejudice still abound in this time. "I am Doctor Andrew Thompson."

The man leaned back in his chair in surprise and looked to his right. "She is sitting in the living room," he said.

Andrew bowed. "Thank you, sir," he said, and walked away. He knew that the attendant was watching him carefully.

He walked into the living room and saw Rowena sitting by the window. His heart pounded his chest as he walked toward her. Her dark hair had turned gray and she had put on a little weight. She was staring out the window but then turned and looked at him. She froze when she saw him and then her face lit up. Her eyes grew wide as her hand went to her face.

"Hi, Ro," he said.

She tried to stand up out of the chair but almost fell back into it. He reached out and pulled her up. They hugged and kissed. She began to cry and he couldn't help but cry too. So many years had passed for her. It was a lifetime since she had seen him. Now he was back in her life. He knew the attendant was finding all of this a bit strange.

She looked up into his eyes. Her hands came free of his, reaching up to touch his face, a smile growing as the tears fell. The dark earnest eyes of the teenage girl he had met so long ago was still there. Now womanhood had given her the kind of comeliness he knew could be dangerous, especially now living in a nursing home. "It has been so long, Doctor Andrew," she said, in a husky voice. "I have grown so old."

He smiled and took her hands in his. "No, Ro," he said, gently. "You're beautiful. You're still the most beautiful --"

She frowned. "I'm desperately unhappy," she said. "I've ended up in here. Why didn't you come back for me?"

"Did you want me to come back?" he asked.

"You showed me the future," she said. "It was so beautiful. I thought we would see more."

"If I would have asked you to come with me, would you have said yes?"

She turned her back to him and sighed, "I would have," she said. "I would have given up everything for you. To go with you in your time ship."

"It wasn't supposed to be like that. I was not supposed to change who you would become. That wasn't fair to you," he said. "You were supposed to write the books about the school that had me go back to the past in the first place."

She turned to face him. "I did write those books," she said. "But you did so much for me. You kissed me, sent me flowers, and showed me your home when you were not going to show anyone else."

"You were very special to me from the first time I saw that graduation picture. I didn't know what to expect. I didn't even know it would work. But I enjoyed my time with you. I just didn't know."

Rowena stepped up to him and again caressed his face with her hand. "I'm an old woman now. I don't know how long I have left. You probably know. But Doctor Andrew, please come back to me."

Andrew took her hand, kissed it, and gave her a big hug. "I didn't know, Ro, I didn't know. The last thing I wanted to do was hurt you. I'm going back to see you."

She smiled. "Oh, Doctor Andrew Thompson, you changed my life, you changed my parents' lives, and you even changed Sarah's life too."

Andrew frowned, staring at her trying to remember. "Sarah? Wasn't she one of your classmates?"

She looked up at him with bright eyes. "Yes, I graduated with her. She came into the time ship. She was very critical of you at first. She even wanted you arrested. But once she realized who you were and your true character, she didn't have you arrested. She changed her opinion toward African Americans."

"Wow," he said. "So she was the one who was going to have me arrested. I wondered who it was. I had no idea any of that had happened."

"There is something else," she said.

"What is that?"

Rowena reached into the pocket of her robe and pulled out a coin. She took his hand and placed the coin in it and closed it just like he had done with her so many years ago. "This coin is not worth anything now, but it will in the future."

Andrew looked at the coin and realized it was the same one he had given to her in the girls' dorm, the one from 2022. He smiled and almost cried at the thought of it. "Wow, this is the coin I originally gave to you."

Rowena nodded and looked at him, longingly. She stood on tip toes and then kissed his lips. "Come back to me. I miss you."

34

Rowena was at home studying for her classes. She was now twenty-four-years-old and had become a math and science teacher at the small school she had graduated from. She felt it an honor to be able to teach there. She had been able to find a house in the community. But on this day she couldn't help thinking about Doctor Andrew Thompson. She had not seen him since her academy graduation six years before when she had gone to the future with her parents. He had not been too happy with her father that day even though her father had later apologized. Her parents thought it was best that she forgot about him and got on with her life. Apparently as time went on she felt they were right. She didn't have any attachments to him. They were both adults and had their own lives to live. She still had a career to think about.

Her parents put her in touch with suiters and even more came by to talk about marriage. She was at that age and her family was concerned about her. She didn't really want to think about it. They were good men, especially Ronald and Samuel, whom she had known all her life. She realized that her time spent with Doctor Andrew had changed the way she related to everyone and she was not interested in marriage. She felt she would never marry at this point. It just wasn't important.

She was sitting at her desk working on papers for her biology class when she heard the sound. It was a sound she had not heard for years; a whistling sound crackling like something was banging against something. Could it be the time ship? She could not believe it. She leaped up from her desk and ran for the door.

She heard the knock and swung open the door to the tall young black man. He still looked the same as he did six years before. She could feel the tears welling up in her eyes. She hugged him tightly.

"Hey Ro," he said.

"I heard the sound of the time ship," she sobbed, "and I couldn't believe it."

"I'm here," he said, looking into her eyes.

"Let me see the ship," she said.

She looked out the door to her left and saw the ship that looked like a palm tree. She smiled.

"It likes trees," she said.

He looked at it. "Yes, it does," he said. "Can I come in? Your neighbors may not be too happy seeing me."

"Yes, you can," she said, as he walked in the door. "It's been so long since I've seen you, Doctor Andrew. I didn't think I would see you ever again."

"I'm sorry about that," he said. "But how about that, you're almost my age now."

"I'm twenty-four. You're still twenty-six?"

"Yes," he said. "Actually, technically, you're older than me because you were born in 1870."

She cocked her head and smiled. "You better be very careful, young man."

He laughed. "I couldn't resist."

"I thought that my father's words, when you took us to your time, insulted you and I wouldn't see you again. I'm so sorry, Doctor Andrew. Both my parents were truly sorry and their attitude towards African Americans changed because of this."

"His words were hurtful," said Doctor Andrew, "but not unexpected. Those were the times. Maybe he was just upset that you had been hanging out with me. But I'm good now. It is good to see you, Ro. You've done well."

"I'm a teacher at the academy now," Rowena said, happily. "Have you taken your ship to other places? What have you seen?"

"I went to see you in the future."

"Me?"

"Yes."

"You saw the day I died?" she said, sadly as she led him into the sitting room.

He shook his head. "Not exactly. It was a nursing home. You were an old woman."

"So you came back now?"

"Ro, you asked me why I never came back," he said, sitting down. "I had lost track of what I was supposed to do. I was supposed to learn more about you for my book. There never was enough time for it. There were always other people around and other circumstances to deal with. Can I talk to you now?"

"Of course, I would like that."

He asked her about her upbringing, her parents and her home life. He asked about her dreams and ambitions. How much she liked teaching and writing. He told her about his life, his parents, his dreams about exploring the galaxy which didn't exactly happen. How he had received his doctorate degree at twenty-five-years-old. They spent the entire afternoon talking. He even told her about his research for the book and his first encounter in the dorm. How nervous he was with the girls, the boys who surrounded him, and then with her. He told her of the research of the dress and the headless mannequins that scared him to death. He even helped her with her work. He was so smart. He even stayed to have supper with her. It was such an enjoyable time to spend with him and she learned so much more about him.

"Ro," he said, "would you like to come with me?"

Rowena looked at him not knowing what to say. "You mean on your adventures in your time ship?" she said.

"I told your future self I had not intended to take you out of time. You have your life and your family."

She could hardly believe it. "You mean I could really come with you?"

"Yes, if you want."

Rowena smiled. She wouldn't want it any other way. She always wanted to travel in the time ship with him. "Yes, I would," she said. "I will officially resign from my post. I'll let my parents know somehow. You're right, my father was concerned about you and me. I don't really know if that has changed much."

"We couldn't have a relationship here in your time, Ro. It wouldn't work. It wouldn't be allowed by your society. But in my time, it could. We could walk and talk together with no problems."

"I would like that," she said.

He leaned forward toward her and kissed her lips. She felt so warm and his lips were so tasty. This was her real first kiss. It was even better than the kiss he gave on her cheek. She leaned forward into him and returned the kiss. She kissed long and hard and held on tight.

They couldn't stop kissing. Rowena felt like she was burning up and it was driving her out of her mind. She had never felt like this before. They stood and held each other tight right there in the sitting room. She even felt him lift her off the floor.

She shivered at the contact, so ordinary for most people, so intimate and extraordinary to her. The simple touch resonated through her. She brought their joined hands up, pressed her lips against them. "I need to feel you, Doctor Andrew. Feel something other than this sharp, brittle chill in the pit of my stomach."

Rising to her toes, she kissed him. She felt him stop breathing, holding himself still, waiting for her to move. "I need your help," she whispered against his mouth. "Please kiss me."

He did, cupped her face between his palms, his lips moving over hers. Oh yes, that was what she'd needed, this decadent distraction. Her fingers twisted in his shirt, tugging it up so that she could run her hands over his abs. Her mouth went dry as she felt perfect, toned muscles flex beneath his brown skin.

Getting out of her dress was never easy but somehow he got it done. She thought he looked gorgeous. He was firm and strong and his brown skin felt like silk. She pulled him down to the floor and ran her hands across his bare torso. It was frantic. They were rolling and nothing could have stopped them. It was like the end of the world. They shuddered to a stop and lay gasping. They were bathed in sweat, totally spent.

They allowed their breathing to return to normal. She leaned closer to him and gazed upon his beautiful form. She felt so good. She felt so warm as she looked at him. She could feel the sweat going down her neck. She wanted to kiss him again.

She stared down at the arm draped over her waist. Dark and sinewy, capable of strength and tenderness. When was the last time Doctor Andrew had been with someone?

They lay there clasped and caressing. She pulled him close, inviting his kisses. Then she got off him and pulled him up. They kissed again as they staggered through to her bedroom. She pulled back the covers on the small bed and they collapsed in. Held each other and fell into a deep afterglow stupor. Rowena snuggled up beside Doctor Andrew and he was playing with her hair. Their hands were lazily caressing and exploring unfamiliar contours. She felt so safe for the first time in her life with him.

35

Rowena did not as Doctor Andrew may have feared, start rummaging around where she should not. She was, of course, human, and such thoughts did cross her mind. Arriving in the future, she stayed the night in his apartment. She awoke the next day in the new world, trying to make sense of the new things around her.

As she was soaping away the grime of the last century and a half in a shower, the idea of roaming around the doctor's apartment did cross her mind. It was truly natural to see what the future was about. Even though it nagged at her, she would not go where she was not to in his apartment. He would eventually show things to her like he did the first time.

But, she reminded herself sternly, she had known good, kind, decent men as well. And, she was certain, Doctor Andrew Thompson simply had to be one of them. Everything about him said so. She had never felt so comfortable with any man so quickly, with anyone – had never been put so at ease by someone she had just met in all her life.

Rowena had been getting an education on what had been happening since she left her time. She learned to access the computer among other things in the twenty-first century. She had missed the end of the nineteenth century, the twentieth and a third of the twenty first. She had a lot of catching up to do, but at least she was adapting. These new clothes felt better also. The clothes were different colors with short skirts. She never liked the old dresses. The clothing was now freer. She could live with this.

Doctor Andrew was careful not to bring her around too quickly. There was a lot to learn but she took it in stride. He had Jennie set up a program where she could see video narrations of the 20th and 21th century right up to the present day. She was getting through the twentieth century and was saddened by all the wars and the suffering. She had read about the Civil War which had just occurred before her birth. That was a bloody war but the twentieth century had greater weapons. She was told there would be some sad moments and happy moments too. She wished her family and friends could see this. Doctor Andrew even promised that they could even use the time ship to visit some of these times.

A lot had happened over the years. The high definition Space Telescope had been put up into space. It was projected along with the space elevator to project man into space, maybe even Mars. Global population was meeting a crisis point with two billion more people on the earth. Supplies were being displaced around the world. The expanding global economy now included China and India with more than 80 million people being born each year. This also affected the national grid with communication being in constant demand for residents and businesses.

The United States of America had begun declining over the last few years as a world power. Because of the national debt, the declining manufacturing base and an overstretched military, it proved too much for the country. China and India continued its growth in technology that it overtook the United States who were unable to compete.

A young woman walked into the lab. She was very pretty with light brown skin. Was she Spanish? She looked at Rowena and smiled. "Hi, I was looking for Doctor Andrew Thompson."

"He is in a meeting right now."

"Can you tell him that Doctor Maria Salazar came to see him?"

"Yes, I can. No problem, Doctor Maria."

Maria looked curiously at Rowena. "You're new here," she said. "I don't think I've seen you before."

Rowena straightened up. "I'm Rowena Michaels, Doctor Andrew's research assistant."

"I didn't know he had an assistant. It's good to meet you."

"I've just arrived," said Rowena, shaking Maria's hand. "You know Doctor Andrew?"

"Yes, we met a few months ago and he is a very interesting person."

"That he is," said Rowena. "I'm still trying to get to know him."

Maria gave her a look. "He can be a very complex person," she said. "He is always working on a special project."

"I know." Rowena wondered if she knew about the time ship. But she didn't mention it.

"Did he tell you about it?" said Maria.

Rowena paused and thought a moment. "The project?" she said. "Yes, but I was told not to say anything. He's not ready to announce it yet."

"Oh," said Maria, looking disappointed.

Rowena thought her explanation sounded plausible. She didn't want to say anything out of turn. If Doctor Andrew was there he could say something but she would just be quiet for now.

"What do you teach?" said Rowena.

"I'm in the nursing department."

"Wow. At one time I thought about that."

"Really? What happened?"

"I went into teaching."

"Now you're in physics?"

Rowena paused, not knowing what to say. She didn't want to dig a hole for herself. She needed to watch her words. "I'm helping Doctor Andrew with some of his projects but teaching is definitely my life goal."

"Well, thank you. Tell him I came by."

"I will, thank you, Doctor Maria." Rowena said, as she left the lab.

It seemed like everyone was a doctor here in the future. Doctor Andrew's friend, Doctor Russell, and now Doctor Maria. She didn't know that women could become doctors but she was learning through the videos that everyone could be what they wanted to be. This made her happy. Now that she was in the future, she wondered what she would do. She was sure that Doctor Andrew would have a plan for her. She would not be alone.

36

Andrew found himself in the midst of an inquiry. He didn't know how he had gotten into this. Life seemed so simple once upon a time. Now things were altogether too complicated. Doctor Winston had called together the Board of Trustees of the college to investigate him. What did he do? Did Winston really suspect that he had a special project going on? And if so, how much did he know?

The inquiry took place in the second story conference room in the administration building. Five members of the Board were present. Andrew sat on one end of the long table and Winston sat on the other.

The college president, Doctor Wallace Abernathy, who had graying dark hair, called the meeting to order and asked Doctor Winston to start his case. Winston stared at Andrew for a few moments. Andrew didn't like the look of this.

"Distinguished members of the board," Winston said, "I would like to prove that Doctor Andrew Thompson has engaged in an illegal private project in his laboratory."

Doctor Abernathy ran his hand through his salt and pepper hair. "Doctor Winston," he said, "you have stated serious charges. What proof do you have to that effect?"

"I know," said Winston, "that Doctor Thompson has been conducting experiments with time."

Andrew's mind was spinning. How did Winston come to that conclusion?

"Time?" said Abernathy. "What do you mean?"

"I mean, Mr. Chairman, that Doctor Thompson has constructed a time machine in his lab where he has made several trips into the past."

The board members looked at each other, curiously. They almost didn't know what to say.

"Doctor Thompson," said Abernathy. "What do you have to say to this?"

Andrew took a deep breath. "Board members," he said, "I do not know what Doctor Winston is talking about."

"You deny all of this?" shouted Winston.

"I have nothing to hide. Nothing is happening. No one is allowed in there after hours."

"Are you hiding something in there?"

"Why would you think that?"

"Are you building a time machine?"

Andrew took a deep breath. "Doctor Winston," he said, sternly, "that was a discussion that happened in my physics class weeks ago. We were talking about time travel and the wormhole found near Jupiter. What's the problem?"

"Is that true?" said Abernathy.

"Yes, the students loved it. They talked about it for the rest of the day I heard. There is no law against that."

"I'm telling you, Mr. Chairman," said Winston, "he has a cylinder in that lab that is a time machine. He's probably even used it and brought people back here from the past."

"Why would he want to do that?"

"Only for his thirst for scientific knowledge."

Andrew shook his head. This was getting interesting. "Those people were wearing periodic clothing for the anniversary," he said. "If you saw them, they were wearing modern day sunglasses. I was even wearing a 19th century suit."

"What do you have to say to that, Doctor Winston?" said Abernathy.

"I 'm telling you we need to look in that lab."

Doctor Sharon Collins cleared her throat. She had dark brown hair. "Doctor Thompson," she said, "if any of this is true, you know that you would be in violation of the ethics code."

"Yes, doctor," said Andrew.

"Any project," she continued, "that is done on college property is the property of the college. We would need to not only see it but sanction it. The college would control the majority of it. This is a very serious charge, Doctor Thompson."

Andrew nodded. "I assure the board members that I have not done anything illegal," he said.

"You do not have a time machine?" she said.

"I do not have a time machine. Time travel is impossible. I have taught it, studied it, and even watched some bad movies but that's it."

One of the other board members spoke up. Doctor Keith Richardson, a balding sixty year old, said, "Doctor Winston, how do you know what's in Doctor Thompson's lab? Have you seen the cylinder?"

Winston stared at Richardson for a moment, obviously speechless and dumbfounded by the question. It was like he had not anticipated it. "I have my sources, Doctor," he responded. "There is a cylinder and it is the time machine."

The board members looked at each other, but no one responded. "Okay, you and the others can go in and report back your findings," said Abernathy. "This meeting is adjourned."

37

Andrew, Rowena and Russell stood in the lab talking about what was about to happen. Andrew filled them in on what the Board of Trustees had concluded. He had always been afraid of this but never thought that it would ever come to it.

"You said you might get into trouble," said Rowena.

"Didn't know it would be like this," said Andrew. "It's like a nightmare."

"He's not kidding," said Russell. "Winston's crazy, but he'll try to prove his case.

"Did he put any bugs in here?" said Andrew.

"Bugs?" said Rowena, scowling.

Russell looked at her. "Those are listening devices," he told her. "They're small, almost undetectable."

"Someone came in here," said Andrew. "I know someone was watching me on my date with Maria."

Rowena stared at him. "You had a date with Doctor Maria?"

Andrew paused a moment. He had almost forgot about it and Rowena didn't know about it. He couldn't afford to get into any more trouble. He nodded. "That was a while ago before I met you," he said. "I forgot you two have just met."

"How did Winston know about the time ship?" said Russell.

"Someone's helping him," said Andrew.

Russell snapped his fingers, "Maybe the guy that was watching you," he said.

"He may be feeding Winston information," said Andrew. "A spy."

"I don't like it," said Russell.

"I don't either," said Andrew. "We're going to have to tread carefully and be smart about this. We're going to have to go to plan B."

"What's plan B?" said Rowena.

Andrew looked at Russell and then at Rowena. "Ro, it would be good if you don't know for now."

Andrew was afraid this day would come. He didn't know it would come so quickly. He decided to do something that would turn this thing around but what could he do? Winston could show up at any time. He would be arrested, thrown out of college, and lose everything that he had worked for.

38

Andrew and Rowena were working in the lab together. He was very happy to have her with him. When she agreed to come and assist him, he didn't know how this would work. But she had adapted to the 21th century life very well. He took her shopping for modern clothing and she just looked great. Those nineteenth century dresses were just too cumbersome.

Doctor Winston walked into the lab with two administrators, Doctor Richardson and Doctor Friedman. Winston looked at Andrew and shouted, "We want to know what is going on in here? What are you working on, Thompson? What are you doing in here?"

Andrew and Rowena looked at each other. "Doctor Winston," said Andrew, "as I told you in your office, and in the inquiry, I'm not hiding anything. Right now we're trying to work on a lesson plan for my class."

Winston walked around the room and even stared at Rowena for a moment. Rowena looked at Andrew with a confused look on her face. "Who are you?" he said.

"I'm Rowena. I'm assisting Doctor Andrew in his work."

"Weren't you wearing 19th century clothing the other day?"

She shivered and glanced at Andrew and then back at Winston. "That was for the school's anniversary," she said.

"She's one of our new physics majors," said Andrew.

Winston frowned, turned and looked at the cylinder. "What's in this big cylinder, Thompson?"

"It's just a special project I'm working on."

"You mean secret," said Winston. "Open it up!"

"Doctor Winston, I assure you that there is nothing ..."

"Thompson, we want to see what's in there now!" shouted Winston.

Andrew looked at Rowena and sighed. "Okay, I guess I'll have to do it."

As Andrew stood up to open the cylinder, Russell Kingston came rushing in and stared at him. Andrew looked at him, and frowned, but took the key and opened the cylinder for all to see. Winston stepped over to look inside and when he did, he saw it was just an empty cylinder.

"No!" Winston shouted.

"What did you expect to find in there?" said Doctor Richardson.

"It has to do with time. That's what I was told. How can this be? All indications pointed to something with time."

"That was a discussion I had in class," said Andrew. "I told you that."

"You better check your sources more closely, Doctor Winston," said Doctor Richardson.

"I think we're done here," said Doctor Friedman. "Doctor Thompson, please excuse the intrusion. We will relay our findings to Doctor Abernathy. Doctor Winston, can I see you in my office."

Winston stormed out of the lab with the two administrators looking very embarrassed. He had thought he had caught Andrew in a violation of school policies but instead it turned and blew up in his face and Winston would never be able to live this down.

Rowena looked at Andrew with a curious look. "What just happened?"

Andrew smiled. "Russell and I did a little switch."

Rowena shook her head, "Switch?" she said. "You mean this was Plan B?"

"I have Andrew's back," smiled Russell. "We had to move quickly because it almost backfired."

"Where's the time ship?" she said.

"My place," said Russell. "We switched a while ago thinking that this would happen. You were right again, buddy."

"Grab a bracelet, Ro. You get one too, Russell. Let's go see the time ship."

Rowena put on the bracelet. "How?"

"Come over here," Andrew said, moving to the back of the lab. "You see this black strip on the floor? Stand on it."

"What is it?" said Rowena.

"It's a transmat. It will take us to the time ship."

"Andrew," said Russell. "You watch too many science fiction movies."

They stepped on the transmat and Andrew smiled. "Just wait till you see this," he said, putting the communicator to his lips. "Teleport to the ship, Jennie."

They disappeared from the lab and reappeared in an apartment. Rowena rubbed her eyes in disbelief.

Rowena gasped. "We traveled to another place," she said.

"This is my apartment," said Russell, a little uneasy on his feet. "Teleporting, huh? I would rather take a bus."

"The bus is not as reliable," said Andrew, jumping off the mat. "I wondered why you put that thing here."

"Well," said Russell, "I would rather make sure that I actually get where I'm going. How do you know that the person who gets reassembled at the other end is actually you and not somebody else with your memories?"

Andrew looked back at him. "You feel like yourself, right?"

They had traveled to Russell's apartment using the transmat pad. The apartment was modest. This was where the party was that Andrew had taken Maria. There was the couch, a couple of chairs and the television. On the far end of the room was the time ship cylinder.

"But how did you do that?" said Rowena.

"I knew that Doctor Winston was suspicious," said Andrew, stepping off the transmat pad. "So Russell and I set up a plan that he would have the original ship here and I would have cylinder B in my lab. As Russell said, we had to move fast otherwise we would have been caught."

"Plan B," said Rowena. "So you moved the ship to the apartment in time so that Doctor Winston thought that was the actual ship still in the lab."

"Correct."

"And we psyched out the spy that he had watching us," said Russell.

"I wonder who he is," said Andrew, opening the door of the ship. "I didn't see him anywhere. I guess that's it."

39

Andrew wanted to do something special for Maria. She had mentioned wishing she could have saved her mother's life when she was thirteen-years-old. Andrew thought if he could take Maria back in time to see her mother and convince her to look after the cancer, maybe she could be saved. Then, he thought, what if he brought a machine that could scan for the cancer and cure it. There was a machine like that at the college.

He went to the health sciences building to see Doctor Dora Sanchez. She was the head chairperson of the department. He wanted to get permission to use the Rosen scanner machine.

"That is a very unusual request, Doctor Thompson," said Doctor Sanchez, as they sat in her office.

"I know, but I would be just borrowing it for a class session. My students need to use it for an experiment."

Doctor Sanchez was a forty-something Latina who was always interested in building students' confidences. She wanted to do everything she could to help them succeed. "Okay, Doctor Thompson," she said, sternly. "When did you want it?"

"I'll come by to pick it up tomorrow afternoon."

"Did you want me to provide some assistance in the move?"

"No, that's okay. I have some help."

In fact, Andrew had drafted the assistance of his friend, Russell. They were going to put it in the time ship. There were a couple of rooms in there that were not being used.

"What did you say we were going to do with this?" said Russell, the next afternoon as they transported the machine to the Center for Theoretical Physics.

"We're going to put this in the time ship without anyone knowing," said Andrew.

"You sure about this?"

"Think you can handle it?"

"Oh, I can handle it. I was wondering how you were going to handle Doctor Sanchez when she finds out what you have planned for it."

"She's not going to find out. I'm going to use it and then bring it back before she knows it's gone long."

"This should be interesting."

They took the machine into the lab and set it up in a room off the control room in the time ship. The object was for a person to lay down on the machine and it would scan for any abnormalities in the body. Andrew laid down on it.

Russell looked at him. "What are you doing?"

"Testing it."

The scanner activated and went over his body revealing a spine out of sequence and an irregular heartbeat.

"I would say you need to see a doctor," said Russell.

"Not until my job is done."

"When will that be?"

"When I'm dead."

40

"What are you going to do now?" said Rowena. "Now that you're free to work on your project, are you going to tell others about it?"

Andrew thought about it. "No, it's still too dangerous. If I let everyone know about it, then Winston will know we tricked him and the college will take the ship from me. I can't let that happen."

"What are you going to do?"

"Now that we have it back in the lab where no one will suspect, I want to do something special."

"What's that?"

"I have one more person to see. She has a date with destiny."

They went to see Maria Salazar. Andrew had an offer which he hoped she would not refuse. He and Rowena walked into her office and Maria was happy to see them.

"Hi Andrew. Hi Rowena," she said. "What's going on?"

"Hi there, Maria," said Andrew. "Sorry to bother you."

"No problem," she cried, leaning back in her chair.

"You've already met Rowena, my assistant."

"I have."

"Maria, I have a proposition for you," said Andrew. "Remember when you said you wished your mother could have gone to the doctor to be cured of that cancer."

"Yes."

"What if I were to tell you that it may still be possible."

Maria stared at Andrew and then at Rowena. "Possible for what?" she said. "This is not funny. What are you talking about, Andrew?"

"I need to show you something, Maria," he said. "And then you can decide. Come with us."

"Where are we going?"

"To my lab."

Maria still had that puzzled look on her face but she stood and went to the lab with them. Andrew could not imagine the thoughts that were going through her mind. She had said this to him on their date before he had even made that first trip in the time ship.

When they reached the lab, she looked around still not knowing what was going on. They walked over to the gray cylinder. Rowena was smiling.

"Maria," said Andrew, "I'm going to show you something that will blow your mind. This will explain everything."

"This cylinder will explain everything?" she said, looking puzzled.

"Remember the special project I was working on?" he said, pulling out the key.

"Yes."

"It's time, Maria. I'm going to show it to you."

Andrew opened the door and when Maria looked inside, her eyes popped out. She looked in and then looked at Andrew and looked into the cylinder again.

"You can go inside," said Rowena.

Maria stepped inside the time ship and looked around. Andrew stepped in and observed her carefully. He noticed she was taking this rather well.

"Well," he said, "what do you think?"

"It's so big in here," she said. "This is incredible. You can go back in time with this?"

"Yes," said Rowena. "I'm from the 19th century. Doctor Andrew came back to see me several times."

Maria stared at her. "What?" she said. "Wait a minute, you're the one from the past that Andrew was obsessed with in writing his book."

Rowena looked at Andrew, and grinned. "So you were really obsessed with me?" she said. "That's why you kept coming back."

Andrew frowned not thinking this would come up. Why did Maria have to say that? "It took me eight years to build it but it works. I lost my best friend who helped me develop it," he said. "Maria, I can take you back to save your mother."

"My mother?"

"Yes, you can save her life."

Maria stared at him. "But that was so long ago, Andrew," she said. "She's dead."

"We can take the ship back," he said.

Maria began to cry. "You would do that for me?"

Andrew hugged her. "Of course, Maria," he said. "If I could give you back your relationship with your mother, all of this would be worthwhile."

"I don't know what to say," she said through tearful eyes.

Andrew released the embrace and held her hands. He stared into her teary eyes. He loved her so much. "Say thank you," he said. "And then brace yourself."

Andrew went over to the control panel. He had also researched her place and time. He set the coordinates for May 8, 2019 just outside Bridgeport, Connecticut. He pushed some buttons and put his wrist communicator to his lips. "Jennie, begin the sequence." He pulled the lever and the ship bucked and moved through the vortex. Maria's eyes grew wide with excitement.

"We're moving," she said.

"Yes," said Andrew. "Hang on."

Maria took hold of the console. "We're going back in time?" she said.

"Yes. I'm taking you back to 2019."

"I was thirteen."

He looked at her and smiled. "Yes, you told me."

The ship made some sounds. It sounded like it was getting closer to its destination. It was slowing down and then everything was quiet.

"I believe we're here," said Rowena.

"Where?" said Maria.

"The clock says May 8, 2019," said Andrew. "This is 19 days before your mother passed away. You need to go to her now, Maria. She's just out there. Your 13-year-old self is away right now.

Go now, dear Maria, and talk to your mother. Tell her that she needs to see the doctor. In fact, bring her back to the ship. We have a machine that can help her."

Maria looked afraid. "I don't know," she said. "I can't."

Andrew took her in his arms. "Maria," he said, softly. "She was the one who encouraged you to go into nursing even if she never knew. Use that knowledge now to save her life. Tell her."

"You can do it, Doctor Maria," said Rowena.

Maria looked at the door and moved slowly towards it. She looked back at Andrew and Rowena. "Thank you," she said, as she went through the door.

Rowena looked at Andrew and went over to him. "That was very nice," she said. "I like the plan. But I don't think the ship's a tree this time."

"Probably not," smiled Andrew. "It might be a large plant. You want to go see what it is?"

"Sure."

Andrew took her hand and they went out the door.

41

Maria stepped out of the time ship into what was her home in 2019 when she was thirteen years old. It was a sunny day outside as the sunlight shone into the house like she remembered. She shivered thinking she was really there.

She walked around looking at the furniture; the flat screen 40 inch television, and the general layout. She would never have believed that Andrew would be able to do this. She had wanted him to open up to her about the project he was working on, but she had no idea about this. He was a genius.

Oh my goodness, I remember this. I'm really here.

"Hello," she said.

"Who are you?" said the woman standing in front of her. This was her mother. Just as Maria remembered her. Her short dark hair was cut close to the neck.

Maria didn't know how to approach her mother or what to do. "I have come to ask you about your health. I'm a nurse."

"How did you get in?"

"Maria let me in," she lied. "I told her this was very important."

Her mother looked annoyed. Maria was getting her younger self in trouble.

"You need to see a doctor about the cancer. It could be a matter of life and death."

"How did you know about my cancer?"

"You told me."

"No, I didn't," she snapped. "I would have remembered that. Did Maria tell you anything?"

Maria looked deep into her mother's eyes. The older woman's eyes looked so sad. She had so much on her mind. She had gone through so much stress. Maria had forgotten how young her mother looked.

"You look familiar to me," her mother said, looking deep into her eyes.

Maria felt the tears coming. "Mother."

The woman stared at her. "What? What did you say?"

"I'm Maria."

The woman shook her head. "What are you talking about?"

"Mother," she said, softly. "I've come from the future. I'm Maria. I've come back in a time machine a friend of mine made. I've come back to save you from dying too soon. I know this sounds crazy, but it's true."

The woman blinked hard. "Maria?"

Maria reached out and took her mother's hand. "There's something I need to show you," she said. "And then maybe you'll understand."

The woman allowed Maria to lead her into the outer room where the time ship was. Andrew and Rowena were standing outside the ship which had turned into a big palm tree plant. Maria's mother looked at it and putting her hand over her mouth, she almost gasped and cried.

"Where did that come from?" she said.

Andrew and Rowena turned to her and smiled.

"Hello," said Andrew. "Sorry we had to drop in on you like this but Maria had to come see you." He walked up to her. "I am Doctor Andrew Thompson and this is Rowena Michaels."

"And that tree is your time machine?" Maria's mother said.

Andrew turned and looked at it and then back at her. "It's not really a tree," he said. "It changes with the surroundings."

"It seems to like trees though," smiled Rowena.

"You were telling the truth," she said to Maria.

"Yes, Mother, I've come back to tell you to see the doctor. But Andrew has something in the ship that could save your life."

"Oh, my dear, Maria," she said, hugging her daughter. "There is?"

"Mother, it's because of you that I became a nurse and took the doctorate program. Now I teach my students how to help others."

Andrew walked up to them. "Mrs. Salazar," he said. "I have a proposal for you. I have a machine that can scan for your cancer inside my ship. We could cure you."

"What?" she cried.

"It's true. The machine will scan for the cancer and then will go about destroying it."

Maria was surprised and elated. Her mother looked at her and she nodded and smiled.

"You want me to go in there?" she said. "In the tree?"

Maria understood her fears. "It looks small on the outside, Mother, but it's really big on the inside."

"You don't have to worry, Mrs. Salazar," said Andrew. "It's going to be fine."

They led her through the door and when she saw the inside of the ship, her eyes almost popped out. Maria knew exactly how she felt. This was totally impossible. Now Andrew was saying that he could cure her. She wondered what it was.

They walked through the control room to another room where a machine was. Maria looked at it and immediately recognized it. She was totally perplexed.

She looked at Andrew. "The Rosen scanning machine?" she said, putting her hands on her hips.

"Yes," said Andrew.

"But how did you get it?"

"I borrowed it." Andrew moved over to the controls. "I'll return it."

Maria stood there staring at him with her hands on her hips. "Really," she frowned. "I'm sure Doctor Sanchez just let you have it."

Andrew shrugged. "I did ask," he said. Then to Maria's mother, "Mrs. Salazar, please lay down on the machine."

Maria's mother looked at her daughter, unsure. Maria squeezed her hand gently. The woman laid gingerly down on the machine and Andrew pushed the buttons. There was a hum and Mrs. Salazar tensed up.

"Don't worry, Mrs. Salazar," said Andrew. "It will be fine. The machine will scan for anything that is alien to the body." After he said that, a light scan went across her body. The machine started making sounds and calculations.

"Stage four cancer detected," it said, in a female computer voice.

It scanned again and this time it isolated where the problem was in the left breast and deep into the bones and arteries around the heart. The machine made more beeping noises and a white light covered her body. Twenty seconds later, the light disappeared and the machine's hum stopped.

"Procedure complete," said Andrew, turning everything off.

"Is the cancer gone?" said Maria.

Andrew checked the controls and pushed buttons. "Computer," he said, "any indication of stage 4 cancer?"

The machine made some buzzing sounds and lights flashed. "No cancer detected in the body," said the computer.

"She's clean," said Andrew.

Maria rushed over to her mother, who opened her eyes and looked up at her future adult daughter. "Mother, are you all right?"

"Is it over already?"

"Yes," she said. "You're cured."

Maria laughed as she began to cry. She hugged her mother knowing that her life had been saved. This had been a miracle to go back in time. This was truly an amazing thing.

42

Sarah Bell walked in the door of her modest little house. At twenty-four, she was currently doing bookkeeping for Jeb Stone's hardware store. When she left Beacon Academy she thought she would go into teaching like Rowena did. But things did not work out. She was happy that she was able to get the bookkeeping job and that Mrs. Miller allowed her to live in this house.

Sarah had moved back to her hometown of Bridgeport, Connecticut. She could have stayed at home with her parents but she wanted to be out on her own. She had a couple of suitors who were interested in her for marriage but they did not work out. Now she just had to resign herself to being alone for now and trying to make a living.

As she smoothed out her dress and sat down to relax, she thought she heard a strange whistling sound outside. She tried to remember what that sound was because it sounded familiar. As she thought about it, she realized that it had to be the time ship of Rowena's doctor friend. Why would he be coming here? She stood up and then she heard a knock at the door.

She went to the door and opened to a smiling Rowena, wearing strange blue and white clothes and a short dress.

"Rowena?" she said. "Is that you?"

"Sarah, how are you?"

"Oh my," Sarah said, putting her hand to her chest. "What happened? What are you wearing?"

"I know," she said. "It's from the future."

"Hi Sarah," said Andrew, walking behind Rowena. "Can we come in before your neighbors see us?"

"Yes, of course," she said, backing away from the door.

Andrew and Rowena came in and Sarah was amazed how well they looked. They had not changed a bit. They walked into the parlor area.

"Doctor," she said, as Andrew turned to her. "I am so sorry about what I did. I know it was a long time ago when we were in academy but I was jealous and confused and didn't understand everything. I was going to have you arrested. I'm sorry."

Andrew smiled. "It's okay, Sarah. No harm has been done. I've forgiven you a long time ago. You don't need to worry yourself."

"Thank you," she said, almost in tears. Andrew walked over to her and gave her a big hug. She felt like a weight had been taken off of her. She felt so much better.

"We have a surprise for you, Sarah," said Rowena.

Sarah released Andrew and looked at Rowena. "Surprise?" What else could happen?

Andrew walked over next to Rowena. "Yes," he said. "This is not just a social visit. We've returned to the year 1894 to ask you something. How would you like to come to the future with us?"

Sarah was speechless. She stood there with her mouth open. What did he just say? "The future?"

"Yes," said Rowena, walking up to her. "Remember when you asked if Andrew had any friends?"

"Yes."

"He does. And we're going to take you there to meet him."

"What?"

"It's true," said Andrew. "His name is Russell. He's my best friend. He's done a lot for me. He has really put his neck out on the line for me many times. I'll take you there to meet him."

Sarah had almost forgot about that request made the day before her graduation. "He's an African American?"

"Yes, he is," said Andrew. "That's okay?"

Sarah smiled. "Oh yes, it is."

Sarah could not believe it. She was going to the future and she was going to meet a man from the future. A few moments before she was thinking how empty her life had been. Now the sky was the limit and anything was possible.

43

"Andrew, what are you talking about?"

Russell was walking with Andrew and Rowena to the lab. Andrew had told Russell that he had a surprise waiting for him in there. Russell could not think of what it could be.

"You'll see when you get there."

They were moving through the Center for Theoretical Physics where there was a lot of activity with the professors and students rushing back and forth. Many of them were checking information on their handheld devices making sure their assignments and projects were finished.

"I'm supposed to be in the Education building right now for a meeting," Russell said.

"Keisha's taking care of that. You'll be okay."

They arrived at the lab and stopped just outside the door. Andrew looked at him, solemnly. "Russell, I want you to keep an open mind," he said. "What I'm about to show you defiles all explanation anywhere so we don't even bother. Take a deep breath. Ready?"

He had no idea what Andrew was talking about but he took a deep breath and let it out slowly. "Andrew, if this has to do with your machine again," he said, "you're in trouble."

Andrew looked at Rowena who almost couldn't contain her excitement. He opened the door and Russell saw standing in front of him on the other side of the room a young, petite, dark-haired woman dressed in a blue nineteenth century dress, smiling at him.

Andrew stepped inside taking Sarah's hand and led her over to the door where Russell stood. "Russell, this is Sarah Bell. Sarah, this is Russell Kingston."

Russell stepped into the lab and faced her. Andrew released Sarah's hand and moved to the side near Rowena who closed the door. "Good to meet you," he said. "You must have come a very long way."

"Just a bit," smiled Sarah.

Russell didn't understand what was going on. "Where did you come from?" he said.

"The same place I came from," said Rowena.

"She was one of the other girls in the picture I showed you," said Andrew.

He blinked. "What? You came from the past?"

"Yes," said Sarah, looking dreamily up into his eyes. "And I've come all this way for you. My goodness, you are so tall."

Russell looked at his friend. "Andrew?"

"Yeah, buddy."

"You went into the past and found me a girl? How is this ever possible?"

"I know her," said Rowena. "I graduated with her. She wanted to meet you."

"That is true, Russell," said Sarah. "I did."

"You did so much for me, buddy," said Andrew. "You put your life on the line for me. Plus, you were always trying to set me up. I wanted to repay you somehow."

Russell looked at Sarah and took her hands. "You came from the past to meet me," he said. "This is a big surprise. Thank you so much." Russell took Sarah in his arms and they hug each other tight. He had never been so happy in all his life. He knew he would make Sarah happy.

44

The Watcher walked into the lab where Andrew and Rowena were working. Andrew looked up and stepped back. This was the man who had been watching Maria and him from the shadows so long ago. He shivered as he looked at the man wondering what he was planning to do. This was the man who had tipped Doctor Winston off on his experiment. Rowena looked at Andrew in wonder as she probably pondered who the man was. The blond man was wearing a dark suit and looked very pleasant.

"Hello, Doctor Thompson," he smiled. "We finally meet. I'm Hank Smith."

"Yes, I've seen you before," said Andrew, cautiously. "In the woods outside the restaurant a few months ago."

"Yes," he said, and looking at Rowena. "And you must be Miss Rowena Michaels."

"Yes," she said, softly.

"Who are you?" said Andrew.

"I'm from the future."

"You mean you're from a future beyond here?"

"Yes."

"So you're a time traveler?" said Rowena. "You're the man from far beyond tomorrow."

"Yes."

Andrew eyed him carefully. "Why did you tell Doctor Winston about me and then abandon him?" he said.

Smith frowned. "He had other plans," he said. "He wanted to have the time machine for himself."

"Why did you contact Winston in the first place?" said Andrew. "You actually talked to him. You then spied on me and now you're talking to us. Isn't that kind of meddling with the time stream?"

"We had to make contact to see what you were doing and to put a stop to it, if necessary."

"What about us? What happens to us?"

"Yes," said the Watcher, looking at the time ship. "What does happen? You have gone back in time frequently to one period and you have plucked a person out of her time stream changing the course of history. Now what do you think should be done to you?"

Andrew gulped, thinking about an intergalactic jail. "It can't be good," he said.

"But I chose to come," said Rowena.

"I know," said the Watcher, "but it creates a paradox. If you go back and take someone out of time into the future, then that would prevent you from going back in time in the first place."

"The book," said Andrew.

"Yes, the book," said the Watcher. "How is that going right now? Plus the books that Rowena was going to write. And then there is what you just did for Maria."

"But we helped her mother," said Andrew. "That was good."

"Maybe," said the Watcher, "but you changed time. There are laws, you know, Doctor Thompson. People using time travel like this – probably without proper shielding, without training."

"You're a time cop?" said Andrew. "You will notice that I'm not doing this for greed or anything selfish."

"True. And that's a good thing," said Smith. "Almost everyone in the universe lives forward. One thing, then the next, then the next. No second chances, no revisiting. Always forward. It's better, in the end." He paused. "And then there's Sarah Bell."

Andrew was beside himself. This man knew everything and he thought Doctor Winston was the problem. "She wanted to meet my friend, Russell."

"But you took her out of her time too. You shouldn't have done that."

"But she came out on her own choice."

"Yes," said Smith, "but it was not for you to give that choice."

"Will we be able to time travel? You can keep an eye on us," said Andrew.

"We will," Smith said, nodding. "We wouldn't want you to go out and meet yourself."

Andrew shook his head. He didn't like the sound of that. "I'm not going to do that."

Rowena looked confused. "How would you meet yourself?"

Smith nodded. "Yes, you could go back in time and kill yourself or even a member of your family."

"But I wouldn't do that," said Andrew.

"Theoretically speaking," said Smith.

"Of course," said Andrew. "You go back and change something but that could endanger your future. It would be a paradox. I wouldn't want to do that. I just want to travel in time."

"You will need to face the Council of the Watchers."

"You mean like a trial?"

"You can call it that. We want to see if you can be trusted traveling in time. You have done some unconventional things so far. But the council will rule."

"So once we meet with them," said Rowena. "We can time travel."

"It's possible."

Andrew shook his head. "What if this council rules against us?"

"Then you will have to stop your travels and dismantle your time machine."

"No way!" Andrew shouted. "This is my machine. This was the idea that Sean and I had. I made it so I could go back and see history. I didn't make it so you can control me."

"I realize that. You can still do what you want. We will review the case and see if you can be trusted."

"What if I refuse to destroy it?"

"If they rule against you and you refuse to dismantle the time machine, your invention will soon be made known to the world and you will have no peace."

Rowena stepped closer to him. "He's makes a good point, Doctor Andrew," she whispered. "Maybe we should hear him out."

Andrew sighed. There was no way out of this one. He was glad Rowena was there to calm him down. "Okay," he said, "we'll do it your way for now. We will meet with your council and await their decision."

"I understand," said Smith. "Good to have you onboard, fellow time travelers."

"I guess your name is not really Mr. Smith."

"Yes, that would be probably correct."

45

Mr. Smith took Andrew and Rowena to see the Council of Watchers. He used a small device which he pressed and they were immediately transported to the council. They appeared in a white room. Andrew blinked hard just realizing that they had moved without the time ship. Rowena held onto him tightly. He felt her shiver from fright. Then he looked off into the distance and saw a figure approaching them. The man looked like he was floating on air.

Not only was the room white, but even the furniture too. The man wore white. Andrew shivered not knowing what this was about. But it was the man's eyes that terrified him. It was like the man was looking right through him.

His feet settled down on the floor and he walked toward them. There was an aura of majesty about him like he was someone of great importance. Andrew tried to stay focused to see what would happen. But inside he was as much a bundle of nerves as was Rowena.

"Why should we allow you to travel through time?" he said.

Andrew cleared his throat. "I have done it a few times and you have seen I am no threat," he said.

The man stared at Rowena. "You took this girl out of time."

Andrew stood his ground. "This girl came willingly."

"That is not the point."

"What is the point?" said Andrew, angrily.

"As you were told by our agent, there are rules. Time had moved on and certain things had happened. You had no right to change that and her destiny. You changed everything because of your research for the book. That is the point, Doctor Thompson, you should never have done that."

Andrew took a breath. "Maybe you're right, but I've spent eight years building it and then I conducted the tests. I do not have any malicious intents with this. It is purely for scientific research."

The man frowned. Andrew didn't know what to make of it. "Very well," he said. "We will discuss this and let you know our decision. You will be directed to a place of waiting."

They were taken to a room where they awaited the decision. Apparently the people wanted to make sure that Andrew and Rowena were to be trusted traveling in time.

"What is this place?" said Rowena.

"Seems like a holding cell," said Andrew, walking in. "It's very white."

"Are we really in the far future? Further than your time?"

"Yeah," he said, sitting on the white bench. "I've never seen anything like what Smith did to us. You saw that other man. These Watchers are definitely in control now."

Rowena sat down. "What do we do now?"

He looked at her and put his arm around her shoulder. "We wait for their decision."

Rowena stood up abruptly and walked over to the side of the room. Andrew saw her go pale. She shuddered. The defenses crashed down. She pressed herself into the corner by the door. Tried to flatten herself onto the wall. Stared into space like she was seeing all the nameless horrors. Started crying like her heart was broken. Andrew stepped over and held her tight. Pressed her against him and held her as she cried out the tension. She cried for a long time. She felt hot and weak. His shirt was soaked with her tears.

His heart felt like a lump of cold wax in his chest. Andrew wanted so badly to tell her that everything would be all right. He wanted to dry her tears and tell her that there was still joy in the world, that there was still light and happiness. But would she hear him?

Andrew knew he had to sound confident. Fear wouldn't get her anywhere. Fear would just sap her energy. She had to face it down.

"It's going to be okay, Ro. I won't let anything happen to you. I care too much about you to let anyone hurt you."

She looked up at him with tearful eyes. "Promise?"

"Promise."

He drew her close to him and hugged her tightly. He didn't know what the final outcome would be but he knew that whatever happened it would change their lives forever. Rowena's life was already changed. He had seen wonders that he never imagined he would ever see. But what would happen to them now?

46

It was hard to tell what was going on. They were able to look outside the complex they were in. It looked like a glorious morning. A bright blue sky, no clouds at all. A very brilliant sunshine. The room area was flooded with light. The view was spectacular. Andrew noticed that it was a city with flying objects like cars. Then he thought, something's wrong.

"This can't be right," he whispered.

"What is it?" whispered Rowena.

Andrew looked at the buildings, tall and straight in the sun. "This isn't the Earth."

Rowena looked at him. "What?"

"We're no longer on Earth," Andrew said. "It looks like it, but it's not." He moved over to where a Watcher stood. "Where are we?"

The tall Watcher looked at him. "You're in our complex."

"We're on another planet, aren't we?"

"Yes," he said, "The original planet ran out of natural resources centuries ago and the remaining people went out into space to search for another home. They found a wormhole that took them to other planets which they explored and colonize. This is one of them."

Andrew nodded. "Amazing," he said. "All my life I wanted to travel to other worlds and see all the wonders of the universe. Here I am now on another planet which no one in my generation will see."

"This is really another world?" said Rowena.

He smiled at her. "It sure is, Ro," he said. "That wormhole that was discovered around Jupiter. That was just the beginning of everything, the gateway to new worlds."

The door opened and Smith came in and looked straight at them. "It's time now," he said. "The Council will see you now."

They were ushered back to the council room where they were met by a group of six men dressed in white. Some had dark hair and others were bald. They also had those glassy eyes. Andrew and Rowena stood in front of them.

"Doctor Andrew Thompson and Rowena Michaels," said the majestic man in white who had greeted them. He was seated in the front. "You have been permitted to travel through time. The Council has concluded that you will not do anything malicious."

Andrew smiled and Rowena was overjoyed. "Thank you," he said. "So we can go?"

The man shook his head. "Yes and no," he said. "You can go but remember that we will be keeping a close eye on you to make sure that you remain honest."

Andrew sighed. He realized that they were being given another chance. "I assure you, gentlemen that you have nothing to worry about. We will be honest."

"In dealing with humans, we have found that there are many who are dishonest. It is not often that we come across someone who can be trusted. But you, Doctor Andrew Thompson, have proved yourself to be trustworthy and we are willing to allow you this opportunity."

"Thank you," Andrew said, bowing. His heart was returning to a steady beat.

"We don't have the time ship," said Rowena.

"That will be taken care of," he said, pressing a disc.

When he pressed the disc, they heard a whistling sound through the wind and the time ship appeared. It kept the shape of a cylinder. There was nothing really to change into. Andrew was happy to see it. He was also excited that he would finally be able to travel the galaxy and time and space.

47

Andrew felt he had dodged a bullet. He had been given another chance to make a difference. He knew what he had wanted to do. He almost thought he had been denied yet another avenue in life just like the space agency. Now he felt relief and he also knew that Rowena was relieved too. She was looking so much better now. He even noticed that she was getting a little color to her face.

They were standing in the control room of the time ship before departure. Rowena was looking at him for guidance. He wanted to make sure that he didn't lose control like that again. No one was going to take his ship from him. Now he could explore as much as he wanted.

"I want to take you to see my parents and then I need to explain to them what this all is."

"They don't know about the time ship?"

"Not a clue."

"This will probably surprise them."

"Most definitely," he said. "We should go to see your parents too."

Rowena paused. "They definitely will be surprised."

"Your father will really hate me."

Rowena shook her head. "My father doesn't hate you," she said. "He just does not understand."

"Should be interesting."

Andrew took the machine to his home on Long Island. He looked around as they stepped outside. This was the region where he had grown up, and he felt that peculiar sense of homecoming all men felt when returning after many months to the scenes of his childhood. Andrew tried to suppress any form of emotionalism, but despise his best efforts, certain things sometimes touched him deeply. It was a nice two story house in the country. Rowena liked the area and the countryside. His parents were middle aged but still working. Yet they had always been supportive of him and his activities. He had to tell them. He went in the evening when they would both be home.

They went up to the front door. Andrew opened the door and walked into the living room. "Hi Mom and Dad," he called.

His parents both came to the door. "Andrew, you should have called to say you were coming," said his father. He stood about five foot eleven with graying hair.

"I know, but this was important. This is my friend, Rowena."

His parents smiled. "Hi Rowena," smiled his mother, hugging her. She was five foot nine.

"Thank you, Mrs. Thompson," smiled Rowena. "It's good to finally meet you."

"Has something happened?" said his father.

Andrew realized that his parents knew that he had kept to himself and had not gone out to meet many women. So this was definitely a surprise to them when they saw Rowena.

"We need to tell you something," said Andrew.

His parents looked at each other. "You got married?" said his mother.

Andrew shook his head and Rowena smiled. "No, we're not married," I said. "But it is something more incredible."

"Really?" said his father. "Better than getting married?"

"It's like a piece of advice Mom gave me," Andrew said, smiling at his mother. "Never back off something you really want to do because you're afraid of failing. You don't want to get near the end of your life and wonder whether you might have succeeded if you'd only tried harder."

His mother nodded. "Yes, I surely did say that."

"I've been working on a special project for the past eight years. Something to do with time and space. I think it would be best if we showed you."

Andrew took them outside to show them the time ship.

"It's a tree," said his father. "Where did this tree come from?"

"It looks like a tree," said Andrew, pulling out his key.

"What is it?" said his mother.

"Brace yourselves, Mom and Dad," Andrew said, putting the key in the lock. "Prepare to be amazed."

He turned the key and opened the door to the massive control room. His parents stood there amazed that a tree could have so much room inside. They stepped in and looked around wide-eyed at the large room.

"You did this?" said his father.

"What is it?" said his mother.

"It's my time ship. You remember Sean Wallace?"

"He was your roommate your freshmen year," said his father. "I remember he was shot."

"Yes," said Andrew, sadly. "We were working on this together. Before he died, he had me promise I would continue the project. So I worked on it for eight years."

"Eight years?" said his mother.

"I put all my schooling to work."

"You sure did," said his father.

"I've traveled to the past."

"I'm from the 19th century," said Rowena.

His mother stared at Rowena. "What?" she said. "The nineteenth century?"

"How about that?" said his father. "You were doing all of this, plus school. This is amazing, son."

"I realize that you two sacrificed so much for me so I could reach my dream. I just wanted you to know about this. But don't tell anyone yet. One of these days I will announce it to the world. You're the best parents ever."

"Thank you, sweetheart," said his mother, hugging him. "We love you."

"We will need your prayers," said Andrew, sullenly.

"This could be dangerous?" said his father.

"Could be," said Andrew. "So many variables. But we'll try to have fun."

"We will pray for both of you," his mother said, hugging him.

They went back inside the house and Andrew showed Rowena around the house. They went into his room. His bedroom hadn't changed much. The framed photo in which he stood between his parents in front of the monitors at the Kennedy Space Center in Florida still commanded attention from the top of his bureau. A photo of the Space Shuttle Atlantis which was now at the Space Center hung over his bed, and a picture of him with his friend, Isabella, at Jones Beach stood under a lamp. Andrew had always been fascinated with the heavens, stars, nebulae, and black holes. He had longed to see what was out there.

"I was thinking about your mother," said Rowena.

"You were?"

"You have her complexion."

"Pretty much."

She smiled. "Pretty. Very beautiful woman," she said, softly. "Do you have American Indian in your ancestry?"

"Someone in the past may have been. I've heard stories."

"I think both your parents have some."

Rowena was fascinated by his room and the pictures. She picked up the one with Isabella. "Who is she?"

"That was a friend of mine from when I was in high school. Everyone thought we were going together but we were just friends."

Rowena smiled. "Did you like her?"

"Yes, I did, but not like everyone thought."

They sat on the bed together and Rowena lay her head on his shoulder. He was very happy she was there with him. So much had changed in his life since he had been home. He had so many dreams back then. Was it really worth it?

"My world used to be so simple," he said. "I knew who I was, and what I was, and what I was supposed to do with my life."

"No," said Rowena, not raising her head from his shoulder. "You only thought you did. Welcome to the real world, Doctor Andrew. Hateful place, isn't it?"

"No." he said. "It has you in it."

They had a delightful supper with his parents and deep down he wondered if he would ever see them again. He wondered why he was so nervous. This was something he always wanted to do. It scared him but he would not let it show and he didn't want to alarm Rowena. Everything would be fine.

48

Andrew was not looking forward to seeing Rowena's parents again. The last meeting was not that good. Her father had said racist things against him when he was going to take them to the future. Her father apologized but Andrew didn't think her father was happy with his daughter being around him.

James Michaels was a product of the times he was living in, no matter how much he may have done for the slaves.

"Do you think your parents will mind me being around?" he asked Rowena.

"I don't see why not," she said. "They've met you."

"It didn't turn out so good before."

Rowena clutched his hand. "It will be fine, Doctor Andrew."

He put in the coordinates and location and the ship reappeared as a elm tree in the yard of the little house near Bridgeport, Connecticut. He allowed her to knock on the door to surprise her parents. The door opened and her mother looked at her, strangely.

"Rowena, what is happening?"

"You like the clothes, Mother?" smiled Rowena, who was dressed in a purple and white uniform.

"They're so different."

"It's what they wear in the future."

Her father appeared at the door. He frowned at them. "What is this all about?" he said.

"Sir," said Andrew, "we're here because there's something we need to tell you."

"What is it?" said her father.

Rowena smiled. "We've been cleared to travel through time, Father."

"Really."

"Yes, sir," said Andrew.

They walked into the house and went into the parlor. Mr. Michaels wanted to talk with Andrew alone and it allowed Rowena to spend some time with her mother. Rowena glanced over at Andrew with some concern but then went with her mother. They went into the other room where they sat down to talk. Mr. Michaels took out his cigars.

"You don't smoke in the future, do you?"

"No sir, we don't."

He took one cigar and sat down across from Andrew. He lit the cigar and looked across at him as if studying him. There was no disdain at all in his expression. Andrew was concerned with the cigar smoke but didn't say anything.

"You're looking good," said Michaels. "You haven't changed."

Andrew laughed, "I guess traveling around in the time ship will do it."

"I always wondered," he said, tapping the embers of the cigar into an ash tray. "Why did you contact my daughter in the first place?"

Andrew took a deep breath. "I had a book to write for the school and when I saw her graduation picture I had to meet her. I had built the time machine and went back to see her. I guess we formed a friendship."

"It seemed like you wanted to court her."

"You want me to date your daughter?"

"Certainly not!" he shouted.

Andrew flinched, but remained calm in his seat. "Sorry about that, sir."

Michaels contemplated him again. "Is what you do dangerous?" he said.

"Probably, but I assure you that I will protect your daughter. I will not let anything happen to her."

Michaels seemed to contemplate that for a long time. Andrew wondered what the man would say to that. "I know," he finally said. "I see that you are a good man. I appreciate what you have done."

"Thank you, sir."

Michaels took a deep breath, and puffed on the cigar. "You know, I worked for the Freedmen's Bureau."

"Really? I read that you ran out of money and resources to help the freed slaves."

"That was unfortunate."

"Reconstruction could have worked. Just think about it. How could a slave, when freed, live a better life? Without a trade or education, the drain on society created hard feelings between them with wealth and those without it. But when people learned a trade and their wages, they not only produced but consumed, making a perfect cycle."

"Did we better their condition? Can they become our political and social equals, just by granting freedom?"

Andrew shrugged. "At least it's a start."

"If Lincoln had lived and we didn't have to deal with that hick Johnson."

"Yeah, well, some things didn't work out."

Michaels paused a moment and then leaned forward. "You could go back and stop Booth from killing Lincoln," he said.

Andrew had thought of that. He could go back and stop the assassination but the problem was that something else would happen. Maybe even something would go wrong. Besides, now he had a time patrol on his tail. "Yes, sir, but I don't think that would be allowed," he said.

"Someone would stop you?"

"Maybe. I've met them."

He sat back and paused again as if contemplating something. "Please take care of my daughter."

"I will."

49

Rowena knew that Sarah and Russell would be in the Education building. That was where Russell worked as a professor and he was Doctor Andrew's best friend. As they walked across the campus, she thought about how her friend, Sarah, met Russell. Doctor Andrew looked at her, curiously.

"What are you thinking about?" he said. She couldn't see his eyes because he had put the sunglasses back on.

She smiled. "I was thinking about how Sarah met Russell."

"Oh yes," he said, "I went back in time to 1888 when you were still at the academy to ask you questions about the book I was writing. You graduated that year with Sarah. We went back to 1894 and picked her up and brought her here to introduce her to Russell."

"That was really incredible because she didn't trust you and wanted you arrested. But you impressed her and she got to like you."

"Yeah, people back then didn't really like black people. I guess we were just strange."

"It really wasn't about not liking black people but we really didn't understand. It was not like I was around blacks every day. We usually stayed away. Blacks were called Negroes back then."

"Well, at least everything turned out okay. You ended up here and seemed to have adapted here in the future. Sarah has really adapted well and the two of them have really clicked."

They reached the Education Building and the doors lid open for them to enter a plush lobby. They took the elevator to the second floor to Russell's office. Rowena didn't know what his schedule was or if Sarah was even there but it was good to be around familiar surroundings after all they had been through.

They walked into Russell's office and found Sarah sitting at the desk in the lobby working on the computer. She had learned the machine very quickly and she felt a purpose in her life. When she looked up and saw them, her face lit up and she jumped up out of her chair to hug Rowena. Then she hugged Doctor Andrew. She looked at him, curiously.

"Doctor Thompson, you really look great today," she said. "Where have you two been?"

"You would be surprised," said Rowena.

"I guess I would with you two," said Sarah. "Where did you go?"

"Another planet," Rowena smiled.

"Really?" said Sarah.

"We were on another planet where we met the Watchers who approved us to travel in time."

Sarah's face grew excited. "That's great."

"Yeah, we can go anywhere. They said that we were honest and could be trusted."

"Wow."

"Yes, it wasn't easy," said Doctor Andrew. "We were put on trial but we passed and now we can travel through time and space without any trouble. The Watchers fixed the machine so we can go to any era, any time."

"That is so exciting," said Sarah.

"Where's Russell?" said Doctor Andrew.

"He's finishing up a class. He should be here soon."

The door opened and Russell walked in. He took one look at them and laughed. Rowena liked him the moment she saw him. She was happy that he and Sarah got along well.

Russell smiled. "You two are back already," he said. "Where did you go?" He hugged Doctor Andrew and kissed Rowena.

"We were picked up by an intergalactic time cop agency and put on trial," said Doctor Andrew. "But all is well now. We can travel anywhere in time and space."

"That's so cool," said Russell. "I guess you will be off and going all over now."

"I think so," said Doctor Andrew. "By the way, you two want to come with us in the ship some time?"

Russell and Sarah looked at each other as if in shock. Rowena did not know anything about the offer but she knew she would love to have them experience what she had. Plus, she knew that Doctor Andrew would enjoy having his best friend with him.

"You mean we could really come with you?" said Russell.

"Absolutely," said Doctor Andrew. "I think you should ride in the time ship. I mean, Sarah has already and you haven't."

"That's true," said Sarah.

"We accept," said Russell. "That would be fun. We can go anywhere?"

"Yeah."

"When do we go?"

"Soon."

Rowena kept her eye on Doctor Andrew. She was so overjoyed that Sarah and Russell would be going with them in the time ship. She didn't know about the offer but she was glad for it.

50

It took a couple of weeks but Andrew finally finished the book on the history of the school. Rowena helped with some of the editing and the facts coming from the beginning of the school. He even printed the picture of the first graduating class of the four girls and presented it to Mr. Johnson, the principal of Beacon Academy. He didn't comment on the incredible resemblance of one of the girls to Rowena. He left the book in the hands of the anniversary committee who were very happy to get this special surprise. Sarah had discarded the 19th century dress for more contemporary colors and clothes.

Russell pulled his air car toward Andrew who thought he should get his car modified. It looked so cool. Russell stepped out of his car and had something in his hand. A ring box.

"An engagement ring for Sarah?" said Andrew.

Russell smiled. "Yeah," he said, "I wanted you to see it. I want to know what you think."

He opened the box and Andrew saw the 24 caret ring. It was beautiful. "That's one great ring," he said.

"Thanks. I want to know if you would stand with me and be my best man."

Andrew smiled. "It would be my pleasure to stand with you, Russell. Thank you," he said. "Sarah will make a beautiful bride."

Russell paused a moment. "What about you and Rowena?" he said. "What's happening with you two?"

Andrew sighed. "I don't know if she sees me like that," he said, looking over at the two girls talking. "I mean I like her but I don't know about a future together like that."

Russell shook his head. "Andrew, you're very smart, but some things you miss. She's crazy about you."

"Really?"

"I see it and Sarah does too," Russell said, looking over at Sarah and Rowena talking just a few yards away. "Don't lose her, buddy. She's very special."

Andrew nodded. They had spent some intimate moments together and she was very comfortable with him. He remembered how she kissed and touched him at her house in 1894. Without question, it was one of the most memorable things that had ever happened to him, and in the end he believed he was fundamentally altered by it. He was not just talking about sex or the permutations of desire, but some dramatic crumbling of inner walls, an earthquake in the heart of his solitude. He had become so accustomed to being alone that he could not think such a thing could ever happen. He had resigned himself to a certain kind of life, and then, for reasons that were totally obscure, this beautiful vanilla cinnamon woman from the past dropped down in front of him, descending down those dorm stairs like an angel from another world. It would have been impossible not to fall in love with her, impossible not to be swept away by the simple fact that she was there. He remembered how she came running to see him play baseball in the field with the boys. How she sent the letter into the future to thank him for the flowers. How they rolled around her house passionately kissing each other. She liked him too. "You're right, Russell," he said, "I'll keep it in mind."

"I'll hold you to it," said Russell.

Andrew looked over at Rowena. "Ro, Sarah, it's time."

Rowena looked over and nodded. The two girls came over and hugged their men before stepping into the time ship. Rowena did look rather nice. Maybe he should consider love. He had had trouble expressing it in the past, but she really did make him feel good. She really brought the love out of him. He cared so much for her.

"So where are we going?" said Rowena, as they stood in the control room.

"There's a place in the future we could go for some rest and relaxation," Andrew said, pressing buttons. "A space station."

"A space station in the future," said Russell. "Let's do it."

"This is so exciting," said Sarah.

Andrew pushed the button and the lights blinked off and on. He pulled the lever. The ship moved and bucked back and forth and they held tightly onto the control panel.

"What is happening?" said Sarah.

"I don't know," he said, hoping the Watchers did not tamper with his ship.

THE END

ABOUT THE AUTHOR

Anthony C. Spence loves science fiction, especially from the 1970s and 1980s on television and films. He has a love for research and has published several short stories and a book. He is a graduate of Atlantic Union College, in South Lancaster, Massachusetts. He currently works for Emory Healthcare and lives with his wife, Tracy, in Atlanta, Georgia.

NOTE FROM THE AUTHOR

Word-of-mouth is crucial for any author to succeed. If you enjoyed *The Man from Beyond Tomorrow*, please leave a review online—anywhere you are able. Even if it's just a sentence or two. It would make all the difference and would be very much appreciated.

Thanks!
Anthony C. Spence

Thank you so much for reading one of our **Paranormal Fantasy** novels. If you enjoyed the experience, please check out our recommended title for your next great read!

My Travels with a Dead Man by Steven Searls

"A compulsive page-turner that contains elements of romance, tragedy, adventure, journeys through space and time, terror, mysticism, and meditation. It's a high-octane, multilayered odyssey that is perfect for readers looking for a little bit of everything."

–INDIEREADER

View other Black Rose Writing titles at
www.blackrosewriting.com/books and use promo code
PRINT to receive a **20% discount** when purchasing.

www.ingramcontent.com/pod-product-compliance
Lightning Source LLC
Chambersburg PA
CBHW011138100726
47898CB00009B/3022